COULHILL SCHOOL

KT-382-346

Praise for *Runestone,*
Book 1 in the Viking Magic series

'I think it was the best book I have ever read. I couldn't stop reading it, so I read it in one night!!!' Becky

'Thanks, Anna Ciddor, I really love your book, I think it's the best in the world. Good luck in the future, but I think you won't need it. Thanks for writing.' Lachlan

'I've read *Runestone* twice, it's soooooooooooooooooooo good. I can't wait till the next one comes out.' Claudine

'Oddo's my favourite character because he's so adventurous.' Robert

'I think it's a great book! I didn't know any of those things about the Vikings, and I found them very interesting.' Hilary

'Very entertaining and absorbing.' Kevin Steinberger, *Magpies*

'I found reading *Runestone* a delight, set as it is against the bare but yet accommodating landscape of Norway in approximately 870 AD. *Runestone* is a novel that not only allows us to see an aspect of Viking civilization but also whets our appetite for more: more about Thora, Oddo and Granny Hulda; more about changelings and runestone magic; more by Anna Ciddor.' Bronwen Bennett, President, Dromkeen Society

As a child, ANNA CIDDOR loved reading, drawing and writing, but she never dreamed of becoming an author and illustrator. It was only when she married and had children of her own that the idea first crossed her mind. In 1987 she decided to take a break from her teaching career and 'have a go' at writing a book. The teaching career has been on hold ever since! Anna is now a full-time writer and illustrator, with over 50 titles published. She based the stories of *Runestone*, *Wolfspell* and *Stormriders* on research into real Viking lifestyle and beliefs.

Anna lives in Melbourne, Australia, with her husband and two children.

In 2003, *Runestone* was chosen as a Children's Book Council of Australia Notable Book and shortlisted for several Children's Choice Book Awards.

To find out more about Vikings and the background to the Viking Magic series, go to:

www.viking-magic.com

VIKING 2 MAGIC

wolfspell

The second book about
the adventures of
Oddo and Thora

ANNA CIDDOR

ALLEN&UNWIN

First published in 2003

Copyright © text and illustrations, Anna Ciddor, 2003
Cover illustrations © Steve Hunt

First distributed in the United States of America in 2007 by
Independent Publishers Group Inc., Chicago

All rights reserved. No part of this book may be reproduced or transmitted
in any form or by any means, electronic or mechanical, including
photocopying, recording or by any information storage and retrieval
system, without prior permission in writing from the publisher.
The Australian Copyright Act 1968 (the Act) allows a maximum of one chapter or
ten per cent of this book, whichever is the greater, to be photocopied by any
educational institution for its educational purposes provided that the
educational institution (or body that administers it) has given a
remuneration notice to Copyright Agency Limited (CAL) under the Act.

Allen & Unwin
83 Alexander Street
Crows Nest NSW 2065
Australia
Phone: (61 2) 8425 0100
Fax: (61 2) 9906 2218
Email: info@allenandunwin.com
Web: www.allenandunwin.com

National Library of Australia
Cataloguing-in-Publication entry:

Ciddor, Anna
Wolfspell; the second book about the adventures of
Oddo and Thora

ISBN 978 1 74114 013 2

1. Children – Norway – Juvenile fiction. I. Title.

A823.3

Designed by Jo Hunt
Set in 12.5 pt Bembo by Midland Typesetters
Printed by McPherson's Printing Group, Maryborough

5 7 9 10 8 6 4

Teaching notes for *Stormriders* are available
on the Allen & Unwin website: www.allenandunwin.com

Secret rune messages

Runes are the letters of the Viking alphabet
(the Futhark).
Runes also have magic powers.
If you unlock the secrets of the rune messages in this
book you will find out *how to make your own*

(the Futhark at the end of the book
will probably come in handy).

To all of you who read Runestone *and sent me letters and emails begging me to hurry up and write the next book: here it is, and it's dedicated to you!*

Contents

1
The hungry month

The milk swished into the bucket as Oddo gave the udder a last impatient squeeze. Brushing against the cow's warm, hairy flank, he reached under the feed trough. His fingers found the hazelnut shells he'd hidden there, and he grinned. Two perfect miniature bowls. Filling them from the bucket of milk, he carried them outside and looked around. There was nobody watching.

Oddo laid the nutshells on the snow and slipped back to the barn. He crouched behind the door and peered round, hardly daring to breathe. Trying not to blink. *This* time he was going to see who took the milk. This time, he was going to wait and watch until they came.

'*Oddo!*' His mother's voice rang out across the yard. 'Oddo, I need that milk. Have you fallen asleep in there?'

'Pig's poop,' growled Oddo.

Grabbing the buckets, he stomped out the door. He tossed a glance at the nutshells, and jerked to a halt.

'I don't believe it!'

In those two seconds his back had been turned, someone had sneaked up and drunk the milk! He bent to check the surface of the snow. There were tiny dimples in the whiteness – footprints no bigger than his little fingernail, just the right size for . . .

'Lost something?' His father's voice boomed behind him and Oddo sprang back guiltily. 'What are you poking round in the snow for?'

Oddo opened his mouth but couldn't think of an answer.

'If I say anything about the Little Folk, he'll bite my head off!' he thought.

His father, Bolverk, was pleased when Oddo used his magic powers to bring rain to the fields, or keep birds away from the seeds, but any mention of the Little Folk put him in a temper. 'You're just making excuses to get out of your chores,' he snapped, when Oddo tried to explain that the Little Folk didn't like him doing ploughing. Bolverk certainly would not approve of him giving them even one drop of the precious milk!

February was hungry month. No vegetables in the garden. No berries or mushrooms in the woods. The wheat sack empty and the nuts all eaten.

Even the wolves were hungry.

As Oddo stumbled to his feet, Bolverk lunged for the door of the barn.

'I told you to keep this shut. You know there are wolves lurking about!'

Oddo scurried into the dairy with his buckets, tilted the wooden lid off the milk vat, and poured in his milk.

'Salt fish for dinner again?' he asked. 'And cheese?'

Sigrid nodded, not bothering to speak. She was panting with exertion as she churned the cream, and her warm breath made clouds of vapour in the cold air of the dairy.

Oddo wondered what his friend Thora, and her family of spellworkers, would be having for their dinner.

In the house-over-the-hill, Thora was leaning over the hand mill, tipping in dried peas and crumbled bark from a pine tree. A cauldron of seaweed simmered on the firepit in the middle of the room, and a salty sea smell wove its way through the gloom. Thora gripped the handle of the mill and began to grind the flour.

'What's that you're making, Thora, a new cure for my creaky old bones?'

'No, Granny, just supper.'

Granny Hulda was huddled in her usual corner, loom clattering and fingers squeaking as she wove spells into her magic cloth.

'Is that a rat?' she quavered, as something small and brown with a long tail scuttled across the floor. Edith leapt out of the way, but Erik dived to catch it. With a hoot of laughter he threw it towards his sister.

'No!' squealed Edith. But it was only a spattering of leaves and twigs that cascaded around her.

'Tricked you!' laughed Erik.

Thora chuckled. Her brother was getting rather good at using his magic to make animals. That thing really had looked and moved like a rat!

Thora was tipping the powdered pine bark and peas out of the hand mill when Sissa, the baby of the family, reached out to grab the side of the mixing trough.

'No, Sissa!' cried Thora.

Too late! The baby's chubby little fingers had already closed on the edge. Thora shrugged and sat back to watch. The mixing trough was made from the trunk of a tree that had been dead many years, but as soon as Sissa touched it, buds sprouted along the hollow trunk. In a few moments, leaves were unfurling all over it.

Thora gave a sigh. 'Now I'll get leaves all through my dough,' she scolded, picking at the tendrils. She added a sprinkle of water to her flour and began to mix.

'Peuugh . . . what a stink!' cried Astrid, striding into the room. 'Whose spell is that?!' She pulled off her cloak and flapped at the fumes rising from the cauldron.

'It's not a spell. It's supper!' cried Harald gleefully.

'Oh,' said Astrid. 'Thora's cooking. I should have guessed.'

'You're lucky someone here can cook,' muttered Thora, 'even if it is only pine bark and seaweed. I'd like to see *you* try!'

But of course she never would. The only useful thing Astrid could do was make spells. It was the same with the rest of her family. Thora looked around the room. Her mother, Finnhilda, was strumming the lute. Her father, as always, was carving a rune. Little Ketil was playing with his magic goatskin hood, making different bits of his body turn invisible . . . If it wasn't for Thora, they'd probably be eating stones for dinner. But then, with their magic powers, all of them but Thora *could* eat stones for dinner, if they wanted. It was only Thora who couldn't do spellwork.

As she kneaded the dough, she heard sounds outside – a metallic chinking and the *thud thud* of a running animal. Everyone stopped what they were doing to listen. There was a scrape, a jangle and the startling bray of a horn.

'I summons you in the name of the King!' hollered a loud voice.

They all looked at each other. Astrid was the first to move. She pulled her cloak on again and hurried down the long passage to the door. One by one, the others followed.

ᚦᛁᛋ ᚱᛚᚾ

2
A proclamation

The whole family headed for the door. As they pushed back the door hangings and stepped outside, little Ketil was holding tight to Thora's hand.

'What is it?' he whispered, gaping at the creature in front of them. It was taller than a cow, with a tossing, hairy head and swishing tail. The animal blew a loud, wuthering puff through its nose.

Ketil twisted himself into Thora's long kirtle.

'It's all right. It's just a horse,' said Thora. 'You've heard of horses. They're in all the sagas about the kings and things.'

She was more interested in the carved sleigh hung with bells, and the fat man in the fur-trimmed cloak squashed inside.

'I summons you in the name of the King!' the fat man repeated. 'Your chieftain, Vigmund the Jarl, sits upon the mound of his forefathers, ready to proclaim the decrees of King Harald the Fairhair, new King of all Norway! You must attend him now!'

The man gave another blast on his horn and a shake of the reins. The horse leapt forward and the sleigh skidded round, sending out a spray of snow. A moment later, it was out of sight.

Granny huffed.

'What a bunch of bird twitter!' she exclaimed. 'I'm not traipsing round in the snow to listen to that sparrow-voiced Vigmund telling me what to do! Who's this Harald Whitehead anyway? Never heard of him!' She stomped inside, her bones clacking angrily.

Runolf frowned, and stroked his long, straggly beard.

'Father,' said Edith, tugging anxiously at Runolf's sleeve, 'we have to go. It's the King's orders!'

'I want to see the King!' cried Ketil.

'The King won't be there, silly,' said Astrid scornfully. 'It'll just be that old Jarl Vigmund dressed up in his rusty helmet and chain mail, thinking he looks important.'

'Nevertheless, I think it behoves us to attend this gathering,' Runolf pronounced. 'Let us attire ourselves in suitable garb.'

To Thora's annoyance, Finnhilda instructed all her

daughters to put on their blue witch cloaks trimmed with cat fur.

'But it makes me sneeze!' wailed Thora.

Runolf and the older boys wound headbands embroidered with runes around their hair, and tied their runestone pouches to their belts. Then they set off for the mound, Runolf and Finnhilda leading, the eight children trailing behind.

Through the haze of gently falling snowflakes Thora could see all the neighbouring farmers heading in the same direction. There was Oddo between his parents, grinning and waving. There was Farmer Ulf and family, and that surly-faced newcomer, Grimmr, who'd taken over the useless, rocky land on the far side of Bolverk's.

They gathered at the foot of the mound, staring up at the Jarl. He was rigged out just as Astrid had predicted, in his old battle gear, looking small and insignificant next to the King's burly Sheriff.

Ulf muttered a comment to his wife, then erupted with one of his loud, hearty laughs, his red-gold beard glinting in the twilight. But as the Jarl began to speak, everyone fell silent and leaned forward, straining to hear. The air was bitterly cold. Thora hugged her cloak tight and felt the cat fur tickle her nose. Hastily, she wrenched the hood off her head. It would be very embarrassing to start sneezing.

'Hear ye!' quavered the Jarl. 'This messenger from

King Harald has put an offer before me: that we acknowledge Harald as our King, or set ourselves in battle against him. On behalf of the folk of this realm, I have promised obedience to the King.' His voice rose. 'So let us raise a cheer to Harald the Fair of Hair, King of all Norway, who will defend our land from foreign invaders!'

The King's Sheriff blew his horn and stepped forward.

'Subjects of the King!' he roared. 'Hear ye this proclamation. That from this day forth all land cultivated and uncultivated, all seas, rivers and lakes in the realm shall be the property of the King. That all who seek to dwell thereon or to fish in the waters thereof shall pay to the King a tax. That this tax shall be in silver, butter, meal, or such other goods as please the King. And that all who fail to pay this tribute shall forfeit their property, land and freedom to the King!'

As he went on speaking, everyone began murmuring in angry voices.

'What's he saying?' hissed Ketil. 'What does he mean?'

'I think we have to pay taxes to the King or we'll be thrown out of our homes!' Thora replied.

'Taxes, what are taxes?' Ketil persisted. 'What do we have to pay?'

'Silver, butter, meal . . .'

'Meal? What's meal?'

'Oh, you know, flour for making bread – ground-up barley or . . .'

'Like our pine bark? Does the King want our pine bark?'

Thora stared at him.

'No, he won't want our pine bark. And we don't have any silver or butter either!' she added. She screwed up her face in consternation. 'How are we going to pay?'

Bolverk's voice boomed above the murmur of the crowd.

'Vigmund the Jarl's a jellyfish!' he rumbled. 'An egg yolk's got more backbone than he has. Only a coward hands over his realm rather than offering battle!'

Thora noticed her father making his way up the mound and hurried after him. Runolf bowed to the Jarl and the Sheriff.

'Sires,' he said. 'I am a poor spellworker, not a farmer. I own no cows, no fields of barley. But, if it please His Majesty, I can inscribe for him runestones of magic power that will win his heart's desire, protect him from harm, bring him–'

'Ha!' snorted the Sheriff. 'Ignorant fellow, do you not know that the King is himself the greatest rune-master in the land? He has the knowledge to speak with birds, the power to quench a fire, and the strength of eight men. He has no need of your paltry scrapings.' He turned back to the crowd. 'At the close of the

Gula Thing, I shall return to collect your tributes!'
he announced. 'Take heed! The King has no patience
with those who do not pay. If you value your home,
your freedom and your property, be sure to have your
payment ready!'

ᚹᛁᛚ ᛒᚱᛁᛟ

3
Bows and arrows

All through the hungry month, Oddo listened to Bolverk and Sigrid anxiously discussing the problem of paying their taxes.

'The close of the Gula Thing is too soon!' wailed Sigrid. 'That's in spring! There won't be any new crops to harvest by then.'

'Even in autumn we'd have nothing to spare,' said Bolverk. 'Everything we grow, we eat – or trade at the market. No, it can't come from the farm.'

'Maybe . . . Could Oddo do something with his magic?' asked Sigrid tentatively.

'Hmm, can you make the grain grow any faster?' asked Bolverk hopefully. Oddo shook his head. 'Well, I don't see how making raindrops or talking to the sheep could get the taxes paid . . .'

That night Oddo noticed his mother counting a few grains of barley out of the sack and hiding them away in a soapstone jar. At supper she gave herself only half a serving. When Oddo tried to take less too, his mother fussed at him, and piled his plate even higher. He felt guilty when he broke off a crumb of bread and cheese for the Little Folk, but he couldn't let them starve. Even though he never saw them, he was sure it was the Little Folk who were eating the offerings he left. No mouse or bird or any other creature could leave footprints like those. And once he'd found a broken string of tiny beads scattered in the snow.

After supper, Sigrid busied herself with weaving and Bolverk settled down to whittle prongs for a new wooden rake. With the crumbs of bread and cheese concealed in his hand, Oddo slipped outside. He stood shivering in the middle of the yard, casting his eyes in all directions, searching for a sign. Was that the twinkle of a tiny lamp, or was it just a star reflected in the snow?

Ever since Thora had told him of the Little Folk, Oddo had been longing to meet them. Now that he knew about them living under the ground, he refused to dig the earth or hoe the fields, however much his father stormed at him. Thora said the Little Folk flew into rages if spellworkers, who should have known better, disturbed their homes. And even though she insisted the Little Folk never let anyone catch sight of them, Oddo believed that one day he would manage to meet them and make friends.

It wasn't going to be tonight, though. He watched till he was nearly frozen, but he never glimpsed so much as the flutter of a cloak or the twinkle of a toe.

Next morning Bolverk noticed the meagreness of the porridge in Sigrid's bowl.

'I won't have you starving yourself,' he growled, 'to fill the belly of that gluttonous swine!' He thumped his fist on the table. 'I'll find another way!' He rose to his feet and headed for the door.

As he pulled the hangings aside, a drizzle of sleet blew into the room. Sigrid hurried towards him with his warm fur cloak, but as she started to pin it around his shoulders he snatched it from her hands and gave a hoot of triumph.

'That's it!' he cried. 'Fur! That's what we can use for taxes.' He pointed at the furs covering the bed and sleeping benches. 'We've plenty of furs. Walrus, bear, seal, fox . . . They should keep His Highness happy!'

'But . . .' Sigrid looked at him in bewilderment. 'We use those furs.'

'So? I'll get some more, woman. I'll go north and hunt!' He turned to Oddo. 'Well, son, do you think you're man enough to come on a hunt with me?'

Oddo stared at his father. Hunting! He'd never shot an arrow in his life.

'Here.' Bolverk stumped to the wall where his bow

and quiver of arrows hung. 'Let's see what you can do.'

But when Oddo rushed across the room and stood next to his father, the great bow towered over his head.

'Hmmph,' said Bolverk. 'I think you're a bit on the short side for this one. We'll have to make you a smaller bow. Come on.'

In the shed, Bolverk headed for a pile of branches stacked in the corner. 'Yew branches,' he muttered. 'Brought them back last time I went to market. Should be well seasoned by now.' He thrust one into Oddo's hand and lifted the lid of the tool chest. 'Hold the lamp higher, boy, can't see a thing!' he bellowed.

Sigrid hurried to clear the table as they stomped back indoors laden with branches and tools.

'Right,' said Bolverk, handing Oddo a knife. 'Scrape off the bark and make yourself a bow. And don't go making a mess of it. Can't get any of that yew wood round here.'

Oddo eyed the long, sharp blade of the knife.

'Make sure you follow the grain!' warned his father, settling down with some birch twigs to shape the arrow shafts. 'If you go against the grain, your bow will snap!'

Peeling off the bark was easy, but when Oddo reached the sapwood he scraped carefully, tiny bit by tiny bit, constantly comparing with his father's bow.

Hours later, bow and arrows were finished. The arrows were fletched with glossy eagle feathers and tipped with real iron. Last of all, Bolverk strung the bow with a twine of flax.

'Right,' he said, handing the bow to Oddo. 'Let's see how good a shot you make!'

It was freezing outside, hard to believe that winter was coming to an end. Oddo clenched his teeth to stop them chattering as he listened to Bolverk's instructions. At last he was told to pick up his bow and aim across the yard at the wall of the dairy. His hands were so numb, he fumbled and dropped the arrow. Bolverk gave an exasperated snort. Flustered, Oddo rushed his first shot, forgetting to take his time to draw and aim. The arrow flopped at Bolverk's feet, just a few paces away.

'You haven't listened to a word I've said!' Bolverk bellowed, kicking the arrow. 'Stand straight, hold your arrow straight. Look where you're aiming! And . . . take . . . your . . . time!' His last words were slow and emphatic.

Then he threw up his arms. 'You can work it out for yourself!' And he stumped off towards the house.

Oddo was tempted to give in. The idea of going inside and curling up by the heat of the fire was very enticing. He looked up at the sky.

'Give me a bit of sunshine,' he coaxed.

As he fitted his arrow to the bowstring, a weak ray of sun broke through the heavy cloud. Slowly he drew back the string till his fist was against his jaw. He sighted along his arm and loosed the arrow. This time it soared across the yard, hitting the wall, bang in the centre, with a satisfying *thunk*!

'Yes!' cried Oddo. He swung around with a grin of triumph, hoping his father had stopped to watch, but Bolverk was already inside.

Disappointed, Oddo crossed the yard to retrieve his arrow. The sun was beating down warmly now and the ice underfoot was turning slushy. He splashed back and took aim again.

Hairydog came out to watch and barked every time he loosed an arrow. She galloped across the yard and tried to use her teeth to pull the arrows out of the wall, but they were sunk too deep.

When Bolverk finally returned, Oddo's fingers were rubbed raw from drawing the bowstring and his left arm was covered with bruises from the rebound.

Bolverk cocked an eyebrow at the sun.

'That your doing?' he asked.

Oddo nodded warily, but Bolverk didn't complain. He was studying the notches all over the dairy wall. 'I think you've done enough damage to that wall!' he said. 'Let's see what you can do with a proper target.'

He took up the spade that was leaning against the barn, carried it to the far side of the yard and jammed it, handle-side down, in a soft ridge of snow.

'Right,' he said. 'Aim at that!'

'But I'll ruin it if I hit it!' cried Oddo.

Bolverk snorted. 'No chance of that!' he said. He took up a watching stance, feet apart, arms crossed.

Oddo felt himself grow nervous again. Hairydog was jumping and yipping with excitement.

'Sshh, Hairydog, let me concentrate,' said Oddo.

The dog stood very still; her hair bristled and her long nose jutted towards the target. Oddo took a deep breath and raised his bow. As he drew back the string, the pain in his fingers reminded him of all the practising he'd done. He pretended the shovel was just a spot on the wall like the targets he'd been setting himself all afternoon. He felt himself grow calm. He held his breath . . . and fired.

He didn't feel the twang of the bowstring hitting his bruised arm. He didn't hear Hairydog's bark of triumph as she leapt forward. All Oddo saw was the arrow soaring through the air, straight and true, and hitting that small square of wood, smack in the centre. The spade snapped in two and the pieces fell to the ground.

Oddo looked at his father.

Bolverk was staring with open mouth. Then he gave a great roar and threw his arm round Oddo's shoulder.

'That's my son!' he trumpeted. 'That's my son! Tomorrow we'll go on a real hunt! Tomorrow you'll become a man!'

4
The hunt

When Oddo woke, the room was dark and cold. No lamps were lit and the firepit held only feeble embers.

'Get a move on,' rumbled Bolverk. 'They'll be waiting for us.' He lifted a stick of charred wood from the firepit. 'Here, blacken your face with this.'

Oddo started shivering as soon as he climbed out of bed.

'You're frozen!' cried Sigrid.

'N-n-no. I'm j-j-just excited,' Oddo declared, worried she'd stop him from going out.

Sigrid wrapped a cloak around him, and handed him a pair of his father's boots stuffed with straw.

'The straw will keep your feet warm,' she said.

'Stop babying him,' Bolverk growled.

Oddo slung his quiver across his shoulder and picked up his bow. Sigrid slipped a lump of yesterday's bread into his free hand. Bolverk strode out of the room and Oddo hurried after him, stumbling in the oversized boots.

The sun was just rising as they joined the group at the edge of the wood.

'Here's Bolverk,' called a voice.

'Who's that tagging after him?' asked Ulf, but he winked as he spoke.

Oddo grinned and held up his bow.

'Today I'm hunting too!' he announced.

The others clapped him on the back.

'A hunter! A man!' they said.

Oddo glowed with pride.

'So are we ready?' demanded Ulf.

'What about Grimmr, is he coming?'

'Nay, he likes to hunt on his own. Doesn't like sharing his kill.'

'Grimmr the Greedy!' said someone, and they all laughed.

But as soon as they entered the wood, everyone fell silent. Ulf was leading, a flaming torch in his hand. Oddo tried to move quietly, walking on tiptoe, but his straw-filled shoes rustled noisily. Bolverk glowered at him.

The hunters fanned out and crept forward, listening intently. Suddenly, they heard the howl of a wolf.

Everyone froze. Ulf held the torch up high to check the direction of the wind. The flame flickered to the right. Ulf motioned all the men to move downwind, then stamped on the torch to put out the flame. The hunters glided out of sight among the trees. Bolverk took Oddo's arm and guided him behind a juniper bush.

'Now don't move and don't make a *sound*,' he hissed. 'And no magic!' he added. He hunkered down and pulled an arrow from his quiver.

The wolf howled again, and Oddo jumped as another howl sounded from the birch trees just beside them.

'That's Farmer Ulf pretending,' whispered Bolverk. 'He's challenging the real wolf.'

There was a pattering of paws and a grey shape appeared between the trees. Oddo had never seen a wolf so close before. It was huge – almost as tall as he was. It had a long nose, like Hairydog's, and it swung its head from side to side, ears twitching.

Ulf howled again, and the real wolf bared its teeth and gave a long, low growl. Its eyes were menacing, cold and green, but when Oddo looked into their depths, he suddenly knew what the animal was feeling. He knew this wolf was the lord of its pack. He knew it was guarding its territory, that it had come, confident in its power, to warn off the strange wolf straying on its land. Now it was sensing danger. Looking proud and fierce, it stood its ground, but the hairs bristled on its neck, and Oddo could feel the fear that was filling its heart.

Out of the corner of his eye he saw Bolverk rise to his feet and lift his bow.

'NO!' screamed Oddo.

He tried to run, yelling and waving his arms. But his oversized boots tangled together and sent him sprawling to the ground. He heard the zing of arrows whistle past and lifted his eyes, expecting to see the wolf lying dead in front of him. But there was no body. The creature was loping off among the trees, one lone arrow dangling from its leg.

Oddo scrambled to his feet and turned to face the hunters, arms spread wide, to stop them firing again. There were roars of anger, Bolverk's loudest of all, as the huntsmen lowered their bows.

Oddo took one look at their furious faces, then turned and fled into the wood.

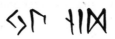

5

A plea for help

The sun was shining, the crab-apple trees were blushing pink and the first leaves were greening the bare branches of the rowan trees.

Thora, basket in hand, was gathering ingredients for the first fresh salad of the year. All around her willow warblers and redwings darted about, singing happily, but Thora moped along with bowed head and heavy heart.

'The Gula Thing is only weeks away,' she reminded herself miserably, 'and I still haven't worked out how to pay our taxes.'

Every night she lay sleepless, tossing from side to side, hearing again and again her father's confident pronouncement:

'Well, as luck would have it, we have one person in our midst who is skilled in practical matters. Thora will find a way to pay the Sheriff!'

Thora had glowed with pride when she heard those words. She'd thought her family only noticed the things she didn't get right. She didn't think they even tasted her cooking or noticed the cleaning and mending she tried to do.

'Of course I'll find a way to pay our taxes!' she'd promised. As long as she could remember, everyone around her had relied on magic to solve all their problems: they used runestones for healing, magic herbs for protection, and spell-woven cloths to save them from danger. Even her best friend, Oddo, used magic to solve his problems. Now, at last, there was something that couldn't be fixed with magic, and she was the one who was going to do it!

Weeks had passed since then, though, and try as she might, she didn't see how she was going to manage it. The season was too early for growing vegetables or herbs in her garden. She didn't have a sheep she could shear, or cows she could milk . . . She shook her head woefully.

The whole family was relying on her, and if she didn't find a solution, they'd be thrown out of their home! Father and Arni would have to join the King's army. And the King would probably force the rest of them to be his servants. For a fleeting instant, the idea of her snooty sister Astrid fetching and carrying for other people was rather appealing . . . But no, it wasn't worth the pain to all the rest of them. It would have been better if the King had wanted magical gifts after all!

Thora spied some new fronds of bracken poking through last season's fallen leaves. As she stooped to pick them, she heard a frantic voice calling 'Thora! Thora!'

A wild boy with a blackened face came racing towards her. Rags streamed from his shoulders, and huge boots flapped on his feet. He fell on his knees and grabbed her arm, knocking the basket with all its carefully gathered leaves out of her grasp. Suddenly she recognised who it was.

'Oddo!' she cried. 'What are you doing?'

He clung to her hand, panting for breath. Dried tears streaked his sooty cheeks.

'You've got . . . to help,' he panted. 'There's a wolf.' He pointed behind him towards the depths of the wood. 'With an arrow. In its leg.'

'Is it chasing you?' she cried.

'No!' Oddo shook his head. 'They tried to kill it! A great . . . big . . . glorious wolf.'

Thora stared at him.

'And you stopped them?' she breathed.

Oddo nodded, looking at her with wide, scared eyes.

'Oh, Oddo.' She sank down on the ground beside

him. 'You're going to be in big trouble.'

'I know. But it doesn't matter about me.' Oddo's voice was fierce and urgent. He had his breath back now. 'We have to help the wolf. We can't leave it running around with an arrow stuck in its leg!'

'What do you want *me* to do?' said Thora. '*You're* the one who can talk to animals.'

'Yes, but you're the one who knows how to heal!' cried Oddo. 'You've got to do something to make it better.'

Thora stared at him.

'Oddo, we're not talking about a cute little pet lamb here! This is a wild animal, probably berserk with pain. I can't just trot up to it and rub herbs all over its sore leg!'

Oddo gripped her hands so hard his nails dug into her flesh.

'You've got to!' he pleaded. 'No one else will!'

ᛏᛚ ᛗᛁᚱᚲ ᛊᛁᛚ

6
The wounded wolf

In the storehouse, Thora considered her shelves of herbs and spices. Some of the chickweed and nettle she'd gathered and dried last summer would be useful. What else? She eyed the packet of myrrh. It came from somewhere far, far away and she'd bought it on her trip to the market. Should she use up some of the precious beads of sap on a wolf? Oddo was hovering behind her, watching tensely. Well, maybe just one drop.

Indoors, there was already a crowd around the firepit. Astrid was boiling up some lichen to make a purple dye for the cloth she was weaving. Granny had come across the fresh leaves Thora had picked for supper and was turning them into a magical potion. Edith was helping both of them.

Thora put her herbs to simmer in a cauldron and sat down to wait. Oddo kicked off his funny big boots, then pulled the shredded cloak from his shoulders. He began to pace around, fidgeting impatiently. Thora looked at the discarded cloak.

'Hey, that's just what I need to make the poultice,' she said. 'See if you can tear it into strips.'

When the herbal mixture was reduced to a dark, gooey paste, Thora scraped it into a soapstone jar. She packed the potion, the bandages and a bag of water into her basket, and they set off for the wood. Oddo walked with his eyes cast down, scouring the ground for any sign that could lead them to the wounded wolf.

At last he saw it, a spot of blood on the snow.

'Look!' he pointed. But the trail was hard to follow. Most of the snow had melted, except in a few shadowy patches.

'This is impossible!' Thora complained. 'We'll never–'

'Sshh!'

Oddo was crouching low. Thora edged towards him and followed his gaze.

A huge grey wolf lay on a bed of rotting leaves, with one hind leg, pierced by an arrow, stretched out awkwardly. Every now and then it lifted its head to lick around the wound, then fell back, whimpering.

Thora forgot to feel afraid. Without even pausing to think, she dashed forward, brandishing her potion and bandages. At the sight of her, the wolf seemed to find new strength. It sprang to its feet, and bared its fangs.

'It's all right!' Oddo called out. 'Calm down.' Thora thought he was speaking to her, but then Oddo brushed past her to face the wolf.

'It's all right,' he said again. 'Thora won't hurt you, Grey Wolf. She's going to make you better.'

Thora couldn't believe her eyes. Oddo held out his hand for the beast to sniff, just as if it were an ordinary dog. And instead of biting his hand off, the wolf lay down and looked at Thora piteously!

Thora realised she'd been rigid as a lump of ice. She took one cautious step, then another.

'Oddo,' she said in a hoarse whisper, 'how are you going to get the arrow out?'

Rubbing the animal's belly, and murmuring words of reassurance, Oddo reached across and tugged at the wooden shaft. The wolf jerked in pain, and let out a howl, but the arrow was out. Blood started to trickle from the open wound. Thora tipped up her water bag, and washed away the blood. Working fast, she made a poultice with the bandages and herbs and bound it tightly round the leg.

'Done!' she announced.

Grey Wolf twisted round to sniff at the bandages.

'Leave it,' said Oddo. 'It will make your leg better.'

The wolf gave a shudder and clambered to its feet. Thora leaped back in alarm.

'It's all right,' said Oddo. And this time he was talking to her.

The wolf licked Thora's hand, then turned to limp away.

'He said thank you!' breathed Thora.

She looked at Oddo. With his soot-streaked face, tousled hair and wide, toothy grin, he looked rather like a wolf himself.

'Are you going home now?' she asked.

The happy look was wiped from his eyes. 'I'll have to,' he groaned.

As Thora watched his dragging feet turn towards home, she wished she could make a potion that would take away his pain too.

ᚾᚠᚲᛁ...

7

Oddo alone

Bolverk strapped on his arsenal of weapons – bow and arrows, dagger, sword, and long-handled fighting axe. Sigrid lowered the lid of the travelling chest.

'Are you going on a hunting expedition or a Viking raid?' she asked.

'Best to be well armed,' Bolverk answered.

'And you're sure you can manage the boat single-handed?'

'Have to, won't I? Somebody's got to stay and look after the farm.'

Oddo hunched on his bed, arms wrapped round Hairydog. He hated his parents speaking as if he didn't exist. They'd treated him like this ever since he'd ruined the hunt. From the moment he'd slunk back through the door, his father had behaved as if he couldn't see him.

What would happen if he leapt up now, and begged Bolverk to take him?

'I could help with the boat!' he thought. 'I can row!'

But then, when they got there, he would have to hunt . . . He chewed his lip and frowned.

'Husband, I wish I could go with you.'

Oddo sat up at Sigrid's words, his heart pounding.

'Mother,' he called. 'Why don't you go? I can look after the farm!' He wished his voice didn't sound so weak and trembly.

His mother glanced at Bolverk.

'I don't know,' she said. 'What would you do about food?'

'I can manage,' said Oddo stoutly. 'I'm not a baby.'

His father grunted and Oddo held his breath.

'Don't be a fusspot, woman!' Bolverk snapped. 'A boy his age should be capable of looking after himself – and keeping an eye on the place.' He tapped the handle of his axe. 'Anyway, if he runs into trouble, Ulf'll be around.' He swung towards Oddo and looked him in the eye for the first time in days. 'So, you really think you can manage, boy?' His bushy eyebrows lifted questioningly.

Oddo nodded, hardly believing what was happening.

'We won't be very long, I suppose,' murmured Sigrid. 'We'll probably be back by the close of the

Gula Thing. When that King's Sheriff returns.'

'What *is* the Gula Thing?' asked Oddo.

'The spring law meeting where people with big heads make laws and tell other people what to do,' growled Bolverk.

'And people with arguments can go to get judgements,' said Sigrid.

'Or *mis*judgements.' Bolverk kicked impatiently at the chest. 'Well, woman, if you're coming, let's go!'

Sigrid's cheeks were pink with excitement as she bundled things into the chest and pinned a fur-lined cape around her shoulders. But as she stooped to kiss her son farewell, her brow furrowed.

'Be sure to cook yourself hot meals,' she whispered anxiously. 'Don't just live on cheese! There's still plenty of salted meat you can boil up. And barley for porridge or bread.'

Oddo nodded as Sigrid hastened to the door and picked up her end of the chest.

'Remember to keep the barn door shut!' Bolverk called back over his shoulder. 'I don't want your friend the wolf dropping in for a snack!'

Oddo could hear his mother murmuring a question, and his father's booming reply. 'He'll be fine. He can always use his magic to get himself out of trouble!'

Then they were out of earshot.

Hairydog jumped off the bed and began to sniff around, as if this room, without Sigrid or Bolverk, was somewhere new and interesting.

Oddo let out a long breath. Shakily, he climbed off the bed and stared at the door in disbelief.

'Father's left me in charge of the farm,' thought Oddo. 'He trusts me!'

He swallowed, trying to quell the frightened feeling squeezing his throat. He tried to feel proud and important.

'I'll start right now,' he decided. 'I'll feed the animals.'

As he headed for the hayshed, he noticed Grimmr in the distance, standing at the boundary fence, eyeing the paddock between them. Oddo bit his lip. The man was surly and unfriendly and Oddo usually kept out of his way, but today . . .

'I'm in charge of the farm so I ought to be friends with the neighbours,' he told himself.

He set off across the paddock.

'Hey!' he called. 'Guess what? My parents have gone away and left me in charge!'

Grimmr didn't answer. He just gave a snort and walked away.

'What a pig!' thought Oddo. He stared at the retreating back. 'Well,' he called, 'I'd better get on with my chores, then.' He waited but there was still no response. 'Nice talking to you!' he muttered and turned back to the hayshed.

It didn't take long to fill the feed troughs. Oddo dusted off his tunic and grinned with satisfaction.

'Now what?' he wondered.

Suddenly, he had an inspiration. With Sigrid and Bolverk away, he had the perfect opportunity to make friends with the Little Folk!

'I'll set up a banquet for them,' he thought, 'with a table and everything. And I'll make it *inside* the house!'

All that day, Oddo worked at his surprise. He managed to split a branch to make a flat top for a very small table, then bored a hole in each corner and pushed in twigs for legs. He told himself he shouldn't feel guilty as he helped himself to Bolverk's tools – but he didn't feel comfortable till he'd finished using them and they were safely back in the tool chest.

In the wood he picked a few sprays of young green leaves for decorating the table. When he made his evening meal, he broke off a piece of dough, rolled it into tiny lumps and cooked the smallest bread loaves he could manage. He used some of the leaves for plates when he set out the banquet. As well as the tiny golden loaves, there were miniature portions of boiled meat, cheese and even a smudge of butter from the last of their supply.

'And now to make sure they find it!' thought Oddo.

He placed an oil lamp on the ground next to the table, stepped outside, and arranged the door hangings so that they hung open a crack. The light beamed out welcomingly and in the middle of the bright triangle stood the tiny table he'd laid.

'It looks like a real banquet!' he thought proudly.

A shadow blocked the light.

'No!' screeched Oddo. He dived back through the doorway, grabbing Hairydog by the scruff of her neck just as she opened her mouth. 'This is for the Little Folk, not you. Come on, hop into bed with me and we'll watch.'

He climbed onto the sleeping bench, hugging Hairydog close. Without the usual snores from his parents' bed, the room felt strange and empty. A cold wind sneaked past the door hangings, rippling the lamp flame, puffing at the embers of the sinking fire, making all the shadows twitch and dance. Oddo drew the fur blanket up to his chin and fixed his gaze on the dark doorway, watching eagerly for his visitors.

ᚦ

8

A mysterious disappearance

Oddo sat up with a shock. What time was it? How long had he been asleep? He turned to look at the banquet table, and let out a howl of frustration. Every crumb of food had disappeared. He'd missed the Little Folk *again*!

Tumbling out of bed, he ran to the doorway and peered out at the grey world. But there was no sign of the Little Folk.

As he stood there, the sky began to lighten. A single warbler let out a trickle of sound, and all around him other birds took up the early morning song. A ray of sunshine caught the side of the dairy, picking out the arrow marks from Oddo's target practice and making the turf roof glow a bright yellow-green.

Oddo took some chumps from the woodpile near the door, and turned back inside to stoke the fire. He needed to warm up! As he blew on the flames, he felt a niggling worry in the back of his mind. Something outside hadn't looked right, but he couldn't think what it was. Frowning, he poured some oats and water into a soapstone pot and hung it over the fire to cook.

'Hairydog!' he called. 'Come here, girl.'

Before they even reached the door, Hairydog started yipping frenziedly. She shot from the house and tore across the yard towards the hayshed. With a shock of disbelief Oddo took in the sight of bare floor and an empty space between the posts. The whole pile of hay for the animals had disappeared!

Oddo could hardly swallow his breakfast. His parents had gone away trusting him to look after the farm. And now, just one day later, he'd managed to lose all the feed for the animals! And he couldn't even comfort himself with the thought that it wasn't his fault, for he had an awful suspicion that this was a mischievous trick of the Little Folk's.

What could he do? Not a blade of grass was visible in the paddock yet, and none of their neighbours would have any hay to spare. How on earth was he going to feed the animals? Already he could hear them mooing and bleating as they called out for their breakfast. He stared dejectedly at the breadcrumbs he was flicking around the table, and thought of Thora making bread from pine bark. Suddenly, he felt a lurch of excitement. If Thora could find food for her family in the wood, surely he could find something there to feed his cows and sheep?

He leapt up, ignoring Sigrid's rule to clean up as soon as they finished eating, and raced out the door. With Hairydog at his heels, he dashed around the wood, searching for something grassy-looking. Not the brown leaves rotting all over the ground. Maybe the pine needles? He was just contemplating a fistful of pine needles when he spied Thora walking between the trees.

'Hey, Thora!'

She looked startled to see him, and as they drew closer he noticed her red, swollen eyes.

'Thora, what's the matter?'

There was no answer for a moment, and he could tell she was struggling not to burst into tears. At last, the words came out in a rush: 'Everyone in the family's expecting me to work out a way to pay our taxes!' she exclaimed. 'And I can't!'

Oddo stood there staring at her in consternation.

'I'll help you think of a way,' he said, trying to sound reassuring. But if Thora couldn't find a solution, it wasn't likely he would!

Thora sniffed, and looked at his hands.

'What are you doing with those pine needles?' she asked.

'I'm looking for something for our cows and sheep to eat,' said Oddo. 'Someone stole all our hay!'

'Stole your hay! Who on earth would do that?!'

Oddo shrugged. He couldn't say anything about the Little Folk after all her warnings to leave them alone.

'Well, you certainly can't give the cows pine needles,' said Thora, sounding more like her usual self. 'That'll make them lose their calves. We'll have to find some of that lichen stuff the reindeers eat . . .' She bustled off between the trees. 'Come on, I think there's some over here.'

Oddo grinned. Thora always had an answer. But then he remembered her tear-swollen face. The problem of the taxes seemed to be the one thing she couldn't solve. What would happen to her family if she didn't find a way to get the taxes? Would they really be thrown out of their home? As Oddo hurried after his friend, he began to wonder if, just for once, there was some way he could help her.

ᛄᚠ ᚲᚵ ᚹᛟᚼᛏ

9
Grimmr the Greedy

The brown curly lichen didn't look a bit like grass or hay.

'It looks like seaweed!' said Oddo dubiously. 'Are you sure the animals will eat it?'

He picked a handful, then looked round for somewhere to put it, and realised he'd rushed out without a basket.

'Here, use mine,' said Thora.

The basket was brimming over by the time they left the wood. Oddo, hurrying towards the barn, heard Thora calling out behind him. He stopped and looked back. Thora was looking across the paddock towards Grimmr the Greedy's farm.

'What on earth are they doing?' she called.

Grimmr and his servants were walking backwards and forwards between Grimmr's property and Bolverk's, carrying lumps of stone. They seemed to be pulling down the fence that divided the two farms, and moving the stones to the middle of Bolverk's paddock, but that didn't make sense. That wall was the boundary between the two farms. Then Oddo realised why they were doing it.

'I don't believe it!' he said.

'What is it?' asked Thora. 'What's happening?'

'That . . . that Grimmr – he's stealing our land!'

'You can't steal land!' said Thora.

'He is. He's moving the fence. He's making our land smaller and his land bigger!' And now Oddo noticed a new shed standing on Grimmr's land, a shed that hadn't been there the morning before. A shed that was full of hay . . . 'And I bet that's our missing hay!' he cried. So it wasn't the Little Folk who'd emptied Bolverk's hayshed after all. It was that bloated, pig-faced . . . Oddo dumped the basket on the ground and turned to Thora.

'He thinks he can get away with it 'cause I'm a kid,' Oddo growled. 'He thinks I can't do anything to stop him!'

Boiling with anger and indignation, he strode across the paddock towards the men. Loudly ringing in his head was Bolverk's scornful criticism of the Jarl: 'An egg yolk's got more backbone than he has. Only a coward hands over his realm rather than offering battle!'

'Oddo, what are you going to do?' called Thora as she trotted behind him.

'I'm offering battle!'

'Oh, Oddo, be careful!'

Oddo came to a halt in front of the new fenceline. Hairydog stood beside him, growling.

'Excuse me!' he called. He meant his voice to sound fierce, but it came out in a squeak. 'I think you're making a mistake! This is our land.'

With a grunt, Grimmr dropped the rock he was holding – almost on Oddo's foot.

'You can't do this!' cried Oddo, jumping out of the way.

'And just how are you planning to stop me, you snivelling earwig?' The man's voice was so deep it seemed to make the ground vibrate. He towered over Oddo, pulling on his fingers so that the knuckles made little explosive snaps. Oddo gulped, and looked back up at him, trying not to show how nervous he felt. From this close, the man looked like an ogre. He was the size of a giant, with a neck as thick as a tree trunk and a gleaming bald head that rose from a vast forest of bushy beard.

Suddenly, Oddo knew what to do.

'I . . . I summons you to the Gula Thing!' he said.

'Huh.' Grimmr regarded Oddo as if he were a pile of

rat droppings he'd found in his bag of barley. 'Little boy,' he rumbled. 'I shall attend the Gula Thing because it pleases me to do so. There will be fine trading there with people from all over the realm. But as for bothering the Law Speaker with your groundless claim – ha! You'll be laughed out of court. No one will pay attention to a puny little insect like you.'

Grimmr lumbered off to fetch more stones. Oddo and Thora watched for a while in disbelieving silence, then turned away. As Oddo bent to retrieve the basket, Thora spoke.

'Will you really go to the Gula Thing?' she asked.

'Yes,' said Oddo firmly. 'And I'll *make* them listen to me.'

'Then I think I'll go with you,' said Thora.

There was a sparkle in her eye and Oddo knew she was having one of her ideas.

'You heard what that horrible man said?' she exclaimed. 'About people going to the Gula Thing to trade? Well, that's what I'll do! I'll sell herbal remedies and earn silver, like that time when we went to market! Then I'll be able to pay our taxes!' She beamed triumphantly. 'And I'll help you make sure those Law Speakers listen! We won't let that old ogre get away with your father's land.'

When Oddo got back to the barn and found that the cows and sheep approved of their new fodder, he began to feel happier. It would be a nuisance going to the wood every day to hunt for lichen, but at least the animals wouldn't starve. And then he remembered how hard he'd worked to make the hay: the hours he'd spent under the summer sun with that heavy sickle, cutting the long grasses and binding them, the pain in his back and the blisters on his fingers – just for Grimmr the Greedy to sneak in during the night and help himself! He wanted to pick up all the boundary stones and hurl them at Grimmr's sneering face!

That day everything seemed to go wrong. When he needed more chumps for the fire, he discovered the wood stack was low. Now he'd have to chop down a tree – a job he hated. He laid his hands against the trunk just the way Thora had shown him, and begged the little elm tree's forgiveness. But even so, when he lifted his axe he felt like a murderer and he couldn't bring himself to attack the tree. Instead, he spent the rest of the day gathering fallen branches in the wood.

By the time night fell, he was too tired to bother cooking. He scraped at the lumps of porridge left over from breakfast, and filled the pot again for the morning. As he crawled exhausted into bed, his eye fell on the little table he'd made the night before. He hauled himself up again, brushed all the breadcrumbs off the big table into the palm of his hand and tipped them on the low table where the Little Folk could reach them. Then at last he closed his eyes and went to sleep.

When Oddo woke next morning he kept his eyes closed and snuggled under the cover, reluctant to start on his chores. Before he could even eat breakfast, he'd have to fetch a bucket of water from the river, relight the fire, grind the barley grains to make the flour, cook the oats, knead the dough . . . And then he'd have to rush off to the wood and search for lichen for the animals.

His belly gave a growl of hunger. Sighing, Oddo opened his eyes and started to push back his cover. Then he stopped, startled. The room wasn't cold. Or dark. And wasn't that the smell of cooking?

He looked towards the firepit. The flames were crackling merrily and the pot was already bubbling and steaming. Bewildered, Oddo got out of bed and padded across the room. Who had lit the fire? His bare foot brushed against something soft and he bent to pick it up. It was small and grey, and looked like a bundle of cobwebs. Was it a spider's nest? As he twirled it in his fingers, admiring the way the threads were woven, he suddenly realised what it was. A tiny hood! He stared at it. There was only one person who could have dropped a hood like that. One of the Little Folk!

'Where are you?' cried Oddo, whirling around. 'Where are you? Let me see you!'

Silence. Nobody answered. The crumbs were gone but there were no more signs of the Little Folk. Oddo laid the tiny hood on the table, and sat down gratefully to eat. As he spooned up his porridge, he gazed round the room, working out what chores he still had to do.

'I've got to fetch the water,' he thought, 'and I'll let the animals know I'm finding them some food.'

He finished eating and picked up the water bucket.

Suddenly, he realised there were no sounds coming from the barn. For a moment, his heart seemed to stop. What had happened to the animals? Had he left the barn door open? Had a wolf got in? Oddo tore out of the house, terrified of what he might find. But when he turned the corner, he found the low door shut, and the cows and sheep all safely behind it, munching in contented silence on a big pile of lichen.

'Oh,' breathed Oddo. This, too, must be the work of the Little Folk. 'Thank you!'

Grinning with happiness, Oddo turned away and took a step towards the river. Then he stopped. Had he just seen a flicker of something moving where it shouldn't have been? He spun round. There was something sliding down the back of a sheep! It was . . .

Banging the door open, he charged across the room.

The sheep bleated in astonishment as his fingers raked her fleece and patted frantically at the scattered lichen. Then he dropped back on his heels, and shook his head.

Could that have been a tiny man he saw sliding down the sheep? Or was it just a falling leaf?

ᚠ ᚱᚲᚻ ᛏᚲ

10
Ulf pays a visit

'Calm down!' Thora exclaimed, irritated that Oddo wasn't the least bit interested in the lichen she'd picked for him on her way. 'I can't understand a word you're saying.'

Oddo took a deep breath and spoke more slowly.

'I think . . . I saw one!' he said.

Thora looked at him in exasperation.

'Saw one *what*?' she demanded.

'One of the Little Folk!'

'Oh, Oddo, you just imagined it because you've been wanting to see them for so long!' said Thora. 'Nobody sees the Little Folk.'

'Well, anyway,' said Oddo, 'they've been here. Look!'

He grabbed her hand and dragged her into the house. He pointed dramatically at the firepit. 'See, they lit the fire and made my breakfast!' He bent down to pick up something and thrust it in front of her face. 'And they dropped this!' Before she had time to see what he was showing her, he was dragging her outside again and round the side of the house. He hung over the barn door and pointed at the floor. 'Look, they left a big pile of lichen. They picked it and brought it for me. Well, what do you think of that?' He turned to grin at her.

Thora stared at the lichen.

'You are very lucky!' she said, but she couldn't help feeling rather peeved. Now Oddo wouldn't need her help any more.

'Oddo!' a voice called. Farmer Ulf was striding across the yard. 'How's our little wolf-friend getting on?' Thora saw Oddo blush with embarrassment. 'Coping all right on your own, hey, coping all right?'

'Everything's fine, thank you,' said Oddo.

'Good, good. So you don't need any help, hey, don't need any help? Just thought I'd pop in before I go.' He rubbed his hands together. 'We're off on a Viking raid. Loading the boat now.'

Thora saw Oddo straighten up, alert, like Hairydog when she heard a strange sound.

'Farmer Ulf,' he asked, 'will you be passing near the Gula Thing?'

Ulf scratched his head. 'Well, yes, I suppose we will,' he said. 'I suppose we will.'

Oddo looked at Thora, and raised his eyebrows. She guessed what he was planning, and nodded in encouragement.

'Farmer Ulf,' said Oddo, 'we need to get to the Gula Thing. Could you give us a lift in your boat?'

'What? You and this lassie?'

Oddo and Thora nodded together.

'And why are you needing to go there?'

'I'm going to sell herbs and earn silver to pay our taxes,' Thora explained.

'And I have to tell the court that Grimmr the Greedy is trying to steal our land!' said Oddo.

'Is he now?' Ulf's merry face grew solemn. 'And do you think the court will listen to you?'

'They'll have to!' said Oddo.

'But who will look after this farm, hey? If you're coming with us, you'll have to leave right now!'

'That's all right,' said Oddo. 'There's someone who'll look after it for me.'

Thora realised he meant the Little Folk.

'But Oddo . . .!' she cried.

'It's fine,' he said fiercely. 'I know they'll do it.'

'Well,' Ulf shrugged. 'We can take you, yes, we can take you. There'll be room on the way up. But you'll need to find your own way back.'

Thora looked at Oddo. They had no choice.

'We'll manage,' she said.

Ulf slapped his thighs. 'Right, see you at the boat, then!' he said. 'Don't keep us waiting.'

There was no time for long farewells and explanations. Thora burst into the long room where her family were all busy at their spells.

'I'm off to the Gula Thing!' she panted. She scooped up little Sissa and planted kisses on her soft cheeks.

'You're not going away again!' wailed Ketil, grabbing her skirt. Thora bent down to give him a hug.

'Just for a little while,' she said. 'I've got to get some silver to pay our taxes.' She glanced around the room. The rest of her family had all stopped what they were doing to stare at her with startled faces. 'You'll have to manage without me again,' she said, glad she wouldn't be here to eat the foul brews her mother would be sure to concoct. It was all very well for the rest of them. They could say spells to save themselves from the lethal effects of poisonous leaves and toadstools, but Thora couldn't do spellwork. She was only good at herbal remedies.

'And how will you be making your journey?' inquired her father, rising slowly and brushing stone dust from his tunic.

'Farmer Ulf is taking us in his longship,' said Thora.

'Oddo's coming too. He's got to ask for a judgement at the Thing. Grimmr the Greedy is trying to steal his father's land.'

'In that case, he must have a runestone to bring him good fortune,' said Runolf. 'I will carve it now.'

'Quick,' said Thora anxiously. 'If I'm too late, they'll leave without me!'

Racing into the storehouse, she crammed pots and jars, herbs and spices into a basket and whirled out the door again.

Runolf was just finishing the stone when she came back, and Ketil held her hand as she jigged impatiently from side to side. As soon as the rune was ready, she grabbed her basket and a small cauldron and dashed from the room.

The sound of Ketil wailing 'Thora! Thora!' followed her through the wood.

When the longship, rocking at its moorings, came into view, she paused for an instant to drink in the sight.

'The dragon ship!' she breathed.

The carved dragon-head, glittering in gold paint, seemed to wink at her in the sunlight, and the flag of black and amber waved from the top of the mast.

Hairydog leaned over the side to bark encouragement. The sail was already unfurling. Ulf, looking grim in a metal helmet with sinister eyeholes, beckoned furiously.

Thora ran down the hill and clambered on board. Before she had time to catch her breath, men were lifting the gangplank and the boat was on its way.

ᚴᚱᛟᛏᛗᚲᛏ ᛋᚾ

11
The Gula Thing

Thora stood in the bow, her arms wrapped round the neck of the dragon, and watched the shore drawing closer. Ahead lay the Thingvöll, flat and treeless, ringed by low hills, and filled with people talking, laughing, selling and buying.

Thora sighed. The men on the longship were sailing off to adventures on foreign shores. She could picture it all in her mind: the silent approach along a river, a peaceful village looming into sight, Ulf giving a signal, the longship gliding up to the bank . . . And then the burst of noise as the Vikings bounded over the sides, yelling blood-curdling cries; the glint of the sun on their helmets, the flash of their swords, the thud of axes . . .

She was jolted from her reverie by a splash of salty water on her face as the anchor landed in the sea. The vision of battle faded, and there in front was the peaceful shore of the Thingvöll.

Oddo and Hairydog leapt over the side and waded through the shallow water.

'Come on, Thora!' yelled Oddo.

Regretfully, Thora turned and picked up her basket and cauldron.

'Why don't you come with us, hey?' said Ulf suddenly. 'Why don't you come with us? We could do with a young lass who knows how to heal!'

Thora stared at him. She could be there! She could be standing on this very deck when the men leapt into battle! And she would see them coming back, laden with their glittering loot. She would be there with her healing potions when they carried the wounded on board, and they'd heap her with praise and gratitude. And jewels and gold.

'Come on, Thora! Hurry up!' yelled Oddo again.

Thora looked at him. He was prancing up and down, his face eager, his hands empty. He'd rushed out of the house, not thinking to bring any food or equipment with him.

'He's as useless at practical things as my family!' thought Thora. She smiled ruefully and turned back to Ulf. 'I'm sorry,' she said. 'I can't come with you . . . this time.'

As she waded ashore she didn't turn back to watch the longship sail away. She fixed her eyes on the Thingvöll, and Hairydog, seeing her approach, bounded off ahead.

The plain wasn't as peaceful as it had looked from a distance. In fact, it was a gigantic, rowdy party. Musicians with horns and drums added their rumpus to the cacophony of shouting, squeals and laughter. Jugglers boldly tossed their flaming torches among the press of moving bodies. Ragged beggars cried for alms, and hawkers cried their wares. Oddo and Thora climbed a hill for a better view. Directly below them, two men, stripped to the waist, were fighting over a deer hide, tugging it to and fro to the shouted encouragement of onlookers.

Nearby, two horses were rearing on their hind legs and lunging at each other with bared teeth and lashing hoofs. Their owners danced around them in a frenzy, prodding them with sharp sticks, yelling and egging them on, while the crowd roared with delight.

The sun began to set and the orange glow was reflected in the snow of distant mountains. Down on the plain, people's faces flushed with pink and the shadows became deep pits of blackness.

'We'd better find a place to sleep!' said Oddo.

They made their way back down the hill, and paused to listen to a storyteller reciting a saga of bold adventurers, kings and battles, ocean voyages and distant lands. Nearby, a boy lit a fire and began to roast a pan of nuts. Oddo drew in a deep, delicious breath.

'Hot nuts! Hot nuts for sale!' called the boy, and very soon he was doing a busy trade.

Oddo leaned close to Thora's ear. 'You'll be selling your herbs like that tomorrow,' he said.

Thora nodded happily.

Gradually the lights of other campfires sprang up as people began to prepare their evening meals. Oddo lit a fire too. Thora filled the cauldron with barley grains and water and they sat down to wait for it to cook. Darkness fell, and the plain became a field of blackness dotted with patches of flame. The rowdy party noises dropped to a quiet murmur.

After supper, Oddo and Thora rolled themselves in their cloaks and curled up close to the fire.

The next thing Oddo knew was the donging of a bell and the light of early morning. He sat up and looked around. People were hurrying from all directions towards a wide ring of stones set up at the foot of the hill. Oddo scrambled to his feet. Hairydog woke too and jumped up, ready to join him.

'No, Hairydog, you stay with Thora,' said Oddo.

Thora was groaning and rubbing her eyes.

'I've got to go right now!' Oddo told her. 'The law court's starting!'

By the time he reached the circle, people were packed three or four deep around it. He tried to squeeze his way in, but the men in front turned and glared.

'What do you want, pipsqueak?' said one of them. 'This is no place for kids!'

Oddo stood on one of the stones and bobbed up and down, trying to see over their heads. One of the Thingmen was climbing the hill. When he reached the summit, he turned to face the crowd and lifted his hand for silence.

'The Gula Thing commences now!' he declared. 'If any man has sought to violate the peace of this gathering by bringing weapons into the sacred circle, let him be banished!'

Oddo's hand flew guiltily to his belt, but with relief he realised he'd left his dagger behind when he'd rushed to join the court.

'If any man should leave the circle because he sets a higher value on food and ale than on this meeting, he shall have no hearing of his complaints.'

Oddo's heart sank. Did that mean he had to go without food all day? But he hadn't even eaten break-fast! He clenched his fists and pressed his lips together. Somehow, he'd have to manage.

'And now I will speak the laws!' said the man. He cleared his throat and began to intone: 'Any man who robs another of his goods shall restore them and atone to the King with the payment of a baug. Now the chattels that may be tendered in payment of the baug shall be as follows. A cow to be given in payment must be sound and whole as to horn and tail and eyes and teats and in all her feet. Sheep to be given in payment must be . . .'

His voice droned on. Oddo found it hard to concentrate. He twisted round and gazed enviously at all the wives, children and tradespeople who didn't have to bother with this. Thora was somewhere in that crowd of lucky people walking, talking and *eating*!

Cautiously, he lifted one foot and tried to wiggle it, but immediately he overbalanced and fell against the man in front of him. The man turned angrily.

'I thought I told you to go away!' he growled.

'Sorry, sorry!' said Oddo.

At last the Law Speaker finished his long recital, and returned down the hill. Now there was a stirring in the crowd – people jostling forward, voices shouting. Oddo, seeing his chance, stepped off his stone, lowered his head, and pushed. Suddenly he felt himself bursting out of the crush, and before he could stop himself he was sprawling on the ground in front of the crowd.

Oddo heard the shouting voices die away. He looked up and saw the Law Speaker pointing at him.

'Little boy, what are you doing here?' boomed the Speaker.

Oddo scrambled to his feet, conscious of everyone staring at him.

'Sire, I'm here to plead a case for my father.'

'And why has your father sent a child in his stead? Has he no respect for the dignity of this court?'

There was a murmur around the circle. Oddo swallowed. 'Sire, my father doesn't know I'm here. He doesn't even know about Grimmr the Greedy. I mean, he doesn't know about Grimmr the Greedy stealing our land. You see, he left me in charge of the farm and he went off in the boat . . .'

Oddo felt his face burning with embarrassment and his voice trailed away.

'Well,' said the Law Speaker. 'If you're here to plead a case, then do so! Summons this Grimmr the Greedy. Summons your witnesses!' The Law Speaker seated himself on his stool next to the other Thingmen and looked expectant. Someone prodded Oddo in the back.

'Go on, don't keep everyone waiting!'

Terrified, Oddo stumbled across the open space of the law court. What was he supposed to say? What should he do?

He stood in front of the row of stern faces and opened his mouth.

'I summons Grimmr the Greedy,' he croaked.

'Speak up, we can't hear you!' roared one of the Thingmen.

'I summons Grimmr the Greedy!' yelled Oddo. He knew his voice sounded like a childish squeal.

There was a stir in the circle and Oddo's heart pounded with excitement as Grimmr stepped into view. The huge man glared ferociously at Oddo.

'Well, insect, where are your witnesses?' he roared. 'I've brought mine!' Two servants stood beside him.

Oddo turned despairing eyes in the direction of the Thingmen. What *were* witnesses?

Then suddenly, there was a shout and a waving arm, and there was Farmer Ulf, pushing through the crowd – together with all the men from the boat!

A moment later they were crowded round Oddo, chuckling at his astonished expression. Ulf gave Oddo such a hearty slap on the back that he nearly fell on his face a second time.

'We decided to turn back. Couldn't leave you on your own, hey?' Ulf muttered in Oddo's ear. And then he turned to the Thingmen. 'We are the witnesses!' he cried. 'And we can tell you where this boy's father, and his father before him, have farmed these fifty years. *That* man,' he pointed at the ugly giant facing them, 'Grimmr the Greedy, who is but lately arrived in the district, has taken land that rightly belongs to Bolverk and his loyal son.' He put an arm around Oddo's shoulders. 'And he's tried to steal my land too!' he added in a growl.

'Do you swear this on oath?' demanded the Law

Speaker. He extended his arm, displaying a silver band sticky with blood. 'This is the ring of oaths, dipped in the blood of sacrifice in the temple! Lay your hand upon the ring of oaths and swear to the truth of your statement.'

Ulf raised his hand and laid it on the ring.

'I swear,' he said.

One by one, the other men did the same.

The Law Speaker lowered his arm.

'And what say you, Grimmr the Greedy?' he asked.

Grimmr snorted like an angry bullock.

'Balderdash!' he bellowed. 'That whining mosquito and his father have no right to call themselves farmers! With their two measly cows and their ten measly sheep and their handful of miserable grains. Why, they don't even have a store of hay for feeding their stock. They just let the land go to waste!'

'You stole our hay!' cried Oddo. 'And our land. And we have twenty sheep, not ten!'

'Quiet!' roared the Law Speaker. 'You have had the chance to plead your case. Should you still be here at sundown when we hold court, we will adjudge your claim. But now your time is ended. Return to your place and let the law court continue.'

ᚠᚱᚮᛗ ᚺᚨᚱᛗ

12
Hallveig

When Thora opened her eyes, all she saw of Oddo was a glimpse of his back as he dashed towards the law court.

'Oddo!' she called. 'I've got something to give you!'

She held up the lucky runestone. But Oddo didn't hear her. Thora shrugged, and dropped it back in the basket. She stood up, brushing off the dried leaves clinging to her long kirtle, and tugged her cloak straight. To her right, a girl was coming out of a tent, a heavy cooking pot in her arms. She looked a few years older than Thora, with delicate features and silky fair hair twisted in tiny braids all over her head. Thora watched her hang the pot over her campfire and begin to stir the contents. The girl glanced up, and smiled.

'Good day!' she called.

'Good day,' Thora answered, and took a few steps towards her. 'My name is Thora,' she said.

'And I am Hallveig,' said the girl. She had a high, sing-song voice. 'And what is your dog's name?'

'Hairydog. But she's not my dog. She belongs to my friend, but he's gone to the Thing.'

Hallveig nodded. 'My father's gone to the Thing, too,' she said. 'Do you want to share my breakfast? There's plenty here!'

Thora and Hallveig sat comfortably in the tent on two folding stools. Hairydog lay at their feet, chewing on bones.

'What are you going to do all day?' asked Hallveig.

'I'm going to make herbal remedies to sell,' said Thora.

Hallveig stopped eating and gazed at Thora round-eyed.

'Are you a spellworker?' she breathed.

Thora looked down at her bowl. What should she say? It was the herbs that did the magic – she just knew how to choose them and mix them so that they healed and took away pain. But people would only buy her remedies if they believed she had magic powers.

She mumbled an evasive answer.

'I can work spells with herbs,' she said.

'Oooh,' squealed Hallveig. 'I know a real spell-worker!'

Thora was embarrassed. She wasn't used to people calling her a spellworker.

'And what about you?' she asked. 'What are you going to do all day?'

'I'm going to look for nettles,' said Hallveig. 'My father's a rope-maker and he needs nettles to make into ropes.'

'We can go together!' cried Thora. 'I can look for herbs while you pick nettles.'

The two girls made their way upstream till the sounds of the Thing died away. Hallveig found a stand of prickly old nettles as tall as she was and began to hack at them with a knife, while Thora picked fresh young nettles, soft, feather-leafed woundwort plants, and the juicy stalks and plump leaves of chick-weed.

'Shall we go back now?' asked Thora, when her basket was full.

Hallveig nodded, out of breath from chopping at the tough stalks. She picked up a piece of twine and began to bind the nettles together.

'Owwww!' She dropped the bundle and danced around, shaking her hand.

Thora snatched some leaves off a broad-leafed dock. 'Here,' she cried, 'this'll take away the sting!'

Hallveig thrust out her hand and Thora wrapped the soothing leaves around her fingers.

'Don't you have to say a spell?' asked Hallveig

'Uh, if you like.' Thora racked her brains, trying to remember one of Granny's chants.

'From nettle sting
Relief do bring!'

she muttered.

Hallveig beamed.

'The pain's gone!' she said.

Back at the camp, Thora lit a fire and hung a pot of water over the flames. Then she spread her cloak on the ground and laid out the soapstone pots and clay jars she'd brought from home. Hallveig put her nettle stalks to soak in a bucket of water and came over to look.

'What's in the pots?' she asked eagerly.

'This is a lotion for soothing squeaky bones,' answered Thora, 'and these . . .'

'Squeaky bones? People don't have squeaky bones!'

'My granny does,' said Thora.

'Hmm, have you got anything more useful?'

Thora picked up a clay jar, pulled out the stopper and showed Hallveig the black smelly goo inside.

'This'll take away the pain if you cut yourself,' she said.

'Auugh, it pongs!' cried Hallveig, 'Put the stopper back in!' She held her nose and backed away. 'Is that all you've got?'

'As soon as this water boils, I'll be able to make more things,' said Thora, feeling rather piqued.

'Make some of those potions that make people fall in love, or give them a long life, or how about those ones that protect you when you're travelling!' cried Hallveig eagerly. 'People will want to buy those!'

'Um, I just make healing herbs,' said Thora.

'Oh.'

The water in the cauldron was beginning to steam. Thora looked round eagerly for customers. An old woman was shuffling past, wheezing and coughing.

'Would you like a herbal remedy?' called Thora. 'I can make you a nice soothing drink to take away that cough.'

The old woman peered down at the pots.

'Got something there for a long life?' she asked.

'No, but I can make you a soothing drink to take away that cough,' Thora repeated.

The woman sniffed wetly.

'All right.'

Thora filled a drinking horn with boiling water and dropped in a few slivers of the ginger root she'd brought from home.

'Here.'

She was just about to hand it to her customer when she caught Hallveig's eager, watching expression. 'Umm . . . Wait a minute.

'Take cough away,
This very day!'

she said triumphantly, then watched anxiously as the

old woman breathed the spicy scent and took a few cautious sips. She drained the horn, handed it back and rubbed her hand against her chest.

'That does feel better,' she said, and began to shamble away.

'Uh, could you pay me a bit of silver?' asked Thora.

'Sorry, dear, don't have any.'

A crowd of giggling girls nudged each other towards the stall.

'Do you want something?' asked Thora. These girls with their plump, rosy cheeks didn't look very ailing.

But one of them was shoved forward by her companions. 'We want to buy some love potions,' she spluttered.

Thora sighed. 'I don't have love potions,' she said. 'Just remedies. I can heal cuts and bruises, a sore belly, an aching head . . .'

'She's really good,' said Hallveig, holding up her leaf-bound hand. 'She took away my nettle stings!'

Her voice trailed off as she watched the customers lose interest and meander away.

'Listen,' she hissed, prodding Thora with an elbow and bending her head close. 'Why don't you just *say* they're love potions . . . or long-life potions . . . or whatever people want? Nobody will know the difference!'

Thora bit her lip. Hallveig was right of course. Nobody *would* know the difference. The Gula Thing would be over in a few days and she'd never see her customers again. She could tell them anything she liked. But she didn't want to earn silver by trickery. She really was a good healer – it was just that she needed patients!

↑ᚱᛋ ᚦᛋᚲ...

13
The duel

Oddo was bored. And hungry. He stood behind Ulf's broad back, pressed so close he could have opened his mouth and taken a bite out of Ulf's cloak. He couldn't see the Thingmen and he was sick to death of the endless declarations.

Suddenly there was a stir of excitement in the crowd in front of him.

'A duel! A duel!' voices were crying.

Four men left the ring with glaring, angry faces and strode towards the pile of discarded weapons. Two of them pushed hazel posts into the ground to mark out a square. The other two armed themselves with shields and swords and took up fighting stances in the centre of the square. One of the duellists was short and stocky with bright red hair. His shield was painted red and yellow and his sword hilt shone gold. Oddo spied the shapes of runes inscribed in the gold. Would they bring this man special fighting powers? The other man was nearly twice his height, but thin and stooped, with a beaky face like an eagle. His shield was black, his sword blade long.

Oddo heard the Law Speaker give the signal to begin. Red Head stood his ground, shield raised, while The Eagle hurtled forward with a murderous howl and plunged with his sword. The long blade smashed into the shield and the wood split and shattered, but Red Head twisted sideways, grabbed another shield from his assistant and charged forward. There was a flash of metal, a loud grunt, and the black shield too was sliced in half.

The Eagle danced around the square, swooping and darting, while his opponent, like an angry bull, snorted and parried.

Then Red Head's second shield splintered into pieces and clattered to the ground. The little man let out a furious bellow and bolted forward, head lowered. There was a sparkle like a leaping flame as his sword hilt flashed in the sunlight, then he stepped away and lifted his arm in triumph. The Eagle was left, staring with disbelief at the blood dripping from his arm.

There was a thunder of cheering. For the first time,

Oddo noticed that people from all over the plain had gathered to watch.

Thora was in the middle of telling yet another young girl she couldn't have a love potion when she heard shouts. She looked up to see everyone running across the plain towards the court.

'Come on!' Hallveig squealed. 'They must be having a duel!'

She dashed off, but Thora paused to load her basket. When she reached the cheering, yelling horde, she pushed her way to the front and saw a tall man sprawled on the ground, blood spouting from his arm. She sprang into action. Heart pounding with excitement and Hallveig close on her heels, she hurried towards the wounded man.

'You'll be all right,' she said. 'I'm a healer.'

She opened a clay jar and tipped the smelly contents into the palm of her hand. 'Here, this'll take away the pain.'

Rubbing it onto his arm, she watched with satisfaction as the colour returned to his cheeks.

'Could some of you carry him to my camp site?' she asked, turning to the crowd. 'Then I could treat him properly.'

As the wounded man was borne aloft, bystanders tagged along, so it was quite a procession that made its way across the plain. By the time the patient was laid beside her fire, Thora had a large audience. She bathed the wound and made a hot poultice of chickweed and myrrh. Then she filled a horn with boiling water and dropped in a few petals of lavendel.

'Drink this,' she said. 'It'll soothe your nerves.'

'Made *me* a drink this morning,' announced a croaky voice. The snuffly old woman was back again. 'Soothed my cough!' She nodded and looked around.

The duellist drank his tea and rose to his feet, flexing his wounded arm experimentally. He beamed at Thora.

'Many thanks, young enchantress, for your kind attention.' He slid a silver snake band from his other arm and proffered it with a bow. 'Please accept this gift in recognition of your service.'

'How about something for my poor legs?' demanded a woman beside him, hitching up a corner of her kirtle to reveal a pair of swollen ankles.

Everyone pressed forward now, clamouring for cures.

'I've got a sore back!'

'Here, what can you do for my kiddie?'

'Hey, wait your turn!'

With so many customers at once, Thora was beginning to get flustered. Then Hallveig knelt down beside her.

'Tell me how I can help,' she said.

Thora pointed at the clay jars. 'If it's a pain, rub on some of that!' she instructed. 'I'll look after everything else.'

She screwed up her face in concentration as she tried to remember the right herbs for every ailment: ginger infusions to cure a cough or clear a fever, cloves for a toothache, rosemarin for headaches, dill seeds crushed and soaked for a good night's sleep . . . She took a deep breath and smiled at her patients.

This was going to be a busy afternoon!

14
The judgement

The long day of arguments drew to a close at last, and the Law Speaker rose to give his judgements.

'The first case is the claim of Oddo, son of Bolverk, against his neighbour, Grimmr.'

Hearing his name, Oddo snapped to attention.

'Here is the decision of the court: all land cultivated and uncultivated is the property of King Harald the Fairhair. But the King, in his generous bounty, allows his subjects to claim tenantry upon his land. It is our judgement that Oddo, son of Bolverk, has a right to claim the land where his forefathers have dwelt for fifty years. But he must lay his claim in accordance with the ancient custom! If he should fail in any deed decreed by that custom, then he shall forfeit that land and it shall become the property of the other claimant.'

Oddo scowled in concentration as he struggled to follow what the man was saying.

'Three days from now, when the business of this law court ends, the Thingmen shall set sail for the land under dispute to bear witness to the land-taking ceremony. Oddo!' The Law Speaker looked in Oddo's direction. 'How many days' sailing is it from here to the land you claim?'

'Uh . . .' Oddo tugged frantically at Ulf's sleeve.

'Two days,' hissed Ulf.

'Two days!' called Oddo.

'So shall it be that five days hence we will arrive at the disputed land. Upon the morning of the sixth day, at the first sign of the sun in the east, shall you light a new fire. And that fire shall be a needfire . . .'

Oddo listened anxiously till the instructions ended, then let out his breath in a sigh of relief.

'That doesn't sound too difficult,' he thought.

The Law Speaker called the next claimant, and Oddo's heart leapt. 'I've finished! I can leave the Thing at last!'

As he stepped out of the ring of stones, he heard a familiar *yip* and Hairydog sprang up to greet him.

Oddo tried to dodge the welcoming licks.

'Hey, Hairydog,' he laughed, 'where's Thora?!'

'Oddo!' Ulf's heavy hand clamped on his shoulder. 'Congratulations! Come and join us for supper, boy. Come and join us for supper.'

'Uh, I'd better find Thora,' said Oddo. 'But thanks anyway. *Down*, Hairydog. Show me where Thora is.'

The dog began to trot across the plain and Oddo hurried after her, feeling anxious. Why hadn't Thora come to meet him? Where could she be? What had happened to her?

Hairydog led him towards the place where they'd camped the night before, but now it was surrounded by a swarm of people. Oddo began to run.

'Let me pass!' he cried, elbowing his way through the crowd.

He reached the front, panting with anxiety. Hairydog was waiting, her mouth open in a grin, but Thora, kneeling among her herbs and jars, didn't even notice him. A strange girl was beside her, and their two heads were close together.

'Thora!' yelled Oddo.

Thora's head jerked up.

'Oddo!' she cried. 'How did it go?'

Before he could answer, a large woman at the front of the crowd turned on him angrily.

'Hey!' she said. 'Wait your turn!'

The other customers rumbled agreement. Oddo shrugged.

'I'll tell you later,' he called. 'When they're gone.'

A tantalizing sizzle of frying onion and fish drifted from a neighbouring booth. 'I'll go and buy something to eat. I'm starving.'

Thora smiled ruefully. 'I won't be long. My herbs have nearly run out. And Oddo!' As he looked back, she held up a bulging pouch. 'I've done it!' Her face was alight with happiness. 'I've made enough silver for the taxes!'

ᚱᛏᚼᚢᛏᚠ ᚲᚠᚱᛒᛋ

15
Words of warning

Oddo glared across the campfire at Thora, chattering with Hallveig. That rat-faced girl was such a groveller, telling Thora how marvellous she was, giving Thora bits of food, offering Thora a bed in her tent. Thora wasn't even looking at him. She was too busy telling Hallveig about her family.

'They're counting on me!' she said proudly. 'Except for Astrid, of course. She never thinks I can do anything.' She grinned and patted her pouch. 'I can't wait to see her face when I turn up with this big bag of silver!'

Then she and Hallveig slipped off their stools and squatted next to Hallveig's father. Erp was shaped like a frog, with puffy eyes, a round belly and stumpy legs.

His voice was almost as high and squeaky as his daughter's, and he spoke in funny jumbled sentences.

Hallveig and Thora spread some plants on the ground.

'Herbs!' thought Oddo sulkily. 'With Hallveig around, that's all Thora can do – show off about her herbs.'

Erp and the girls picked up stones and started thumping the plants.

Hairydog, who'd been dozing, opened startled eyes and scrambled to her feet.

'Hairydog, you've got the right idea,' said Oddo. He stood up too, knocking over his stool so that it clattered noisily to the ground. 'I'm going to find Ulf,' he announced.

Thora glanced his way at last. 'Hang on!' she cried. 'You didn't tell us what the law court said.' She laid down her stone and gestured to the others to stop their banging. 'What was the judgement?'

'You're not really interested,' said Oddo.

'Oh Oddo, don't be so huffy. Tell!'

'I heard it,' piped Hallveig's father. 'I'll tell, if Oddo won't. '

Oddo glared at him.

'They said I have to do a ceremony to claim the land back,' growled Oddo. 'I have to carry a burning torch around the boundaries and light a few bonfires on my way – and get back again before the sun sets and the fires go out. It doesn't sound too difficult.'

As he spoke, he pictured himself parading round the land, a flaming torch in his hand. He heard the cheers of the watching crowd when he made it back to the starting point, and his parents' exclamations when they arrived home and found out what their son had done to save the farm.

His happy imaginings were interrupted by Hallveig's father.

'But the needfire!' squeaked Erp. 'The torch you carry, it must by a needfire be lit. Know you what a needfire is?'

Uneasily, Oddo shook his head.

'Explain it I can. A fire it is that you light by rubbing two sticks together. To use a flint and steel you are not allowed, nor a flame from your hearth fire.'

'What?!' Oddo stared at him. 'But that's impossible. You can't light a fire just by rubbing two sticks together!'

'A bit of doing it takes,' said Erp, nodding and smiling. 'But possible it is. So fast you rub them, they get hot enough to burn, see?'

'But what if I can't?' asked Oddo.

Erp tutted his tongue.

'Then lose the land, you do,' he said. 'And Grimmr the Greedy, he wins it!'

To Oddo's disgust, Thora decided to spend the night in Hallveig's tent. Next morning he was mooching about on his own, watching Ulf and the others prepare to set sail, when Thora came dancing along the shingle towards him.

She was followed by Hallveig and the round, froggy figure of Erp.

'Look!' cried Thora.

She held out her basket with something green coiled inside it. For a moment Oddo thought it was a serpent.

'What is it?!'

'A present from Hallveig and her father,' said Thora. 'It's the rope Erp made last night from those nettle stalks.' She lifted up the long green plait. 'Wasn't it kind of him to give it to us?'

Oddo felt his cheeks flush, remembering all the mean things he'd thought about Hallveig and Erp.

But before he could say anything, Ulf called from the boat.

'How . . . are you two . . . getting back home?' he puffed, hauling on a line.

'On foot,' answered Oddo.

'On foot!' Ulf paused and lifted one arm to wipe his brow with his sleeve. 'It's a long way on foot! A long way! The coastline here's more jagged than a wolf's teeth . . . In a boat you don't get caught 'cause you can sail out to sea. But on land . . .' He tutted and shook his head. 'You've got to get round fjords and bogs and mountains. The track winds all over the place!

And there are bears . . . and wolves.'

A gust of wind made the rigging twang. 'You should find another boat to take you home!' he called. He waved and grabbed the steering oar as the sail billowed.

On shore, the four figures watched in silence as the boat glided away.

Thora looked at Oddo.

'We'll be fine,' she said.

Oddo nodded. 'Come on. We've got five days to get home.'

'Fare you well!' cried Hallveig, wrapping her arms round Thora's neck.

'Ooh,' squeaked Erp, and held up his hand. 'Forgot I did last night to tell you something more! When home you get, take care no fire to light!'

'Why not?'

'A needfire you cannot light if any other fire in your house or land can be found!' warned Erp.

'I'll remember,' promised Oddo.

'Ha!' said a voice above his head. Oddo spun round in surprise. Grimmr, seated on a horse, was leering down at him.

'Travelling on foot?' asked Grimmr.

Oddo gulped. That grin looked more menacing than Grimmr's usual scowl.

'Yes,' he answered warily. 'We're walking.'

'Giving me the chance to get home first, eh? Isn't that convenient?' Grimmr spurred his horse and sped away.

'Now, what did he mean by that?' muttered Oddo.

ᚦᛁᛋ ᚱᛚᚾ

16
Into the forest

Trees crowded the path. Branches, furred with moss, reached over their heads and the wrinkled bark looked like gnarled, peering faces, sprouting the bushy beards of ferns. There was a smell of rot and dampness. Hairy-dog sniffed round the lumpy roots, then darted ahead, eager to explore.

A stream trickled across the path, so clear they could see every stripy pebble lying on the bottom.

'Look!' whispered Oddo.

An otter was paddling upstream, its sleek head poking above the water. Suddenly it dived, then bobbed up again brandishing a big fish. Thora giggled as it rolled onto its back and proceeded to make a leisurely meal, holding the fish on its chest with its two front paws.

'That's a good idea!' said Oddo. 'Want some fish for lunch?' He pulled off his shoes and waded into the stream. 'Ouch, the water's freezing!'

'I'll find some sticks,' called Thora. 'Give me the flint and steel and I'll light a fire!'

Oddo tossed her his pouch, then grabbed at a big fat fish as it glided past. He touched it, but couldn't get a grip, and it flicked away.

'Poop!' said Oddo.

The next fish he spied was a perch, with a long spiny fin down its back. He snatched at it, but the perch just flattened its fin and dived out of reach.

'They're too slippery!' he exclaimed in frustration. He climbed out of the water and flopped onto the bank. 'They just pop out of my fingers before I can get a grip.'

'You need to be as quick as an otter!' said Thora.

There was a pause. The two friends looked at each other.

'Well, why not?' said Thora. 'Did you bring a wand?'

Oddo shook his head. 'I haven't done a shape-change since last summer, when I turned into that seal,' he said.

'Well, then, we'll just have to make one,' said Thora. She frowned as she faced the forest again. 'We'll need something scented, like that juniper branch we used last time. And some flowers . . . That'll be tricky, there's nothing much in bloom yet!'

A few minutes later, Thora was arranging a handful

of tight green dandelion buds in a ring. Oddo found a hazel twig for the wand and placed it in the centre. He lit the end of a pine branch for incense and held it over his head. The pine resin filled the air with scented smoke, but as the pine needles caught fire, each one exploded in a shower of sparks. Thora hastily backed away and Oddo held up his other arm to shield his face.

'Quick, say the spell you made up last time,' said Thora.

'Magic from the ground, magic from the air
Touch this little twig, leave your power there!'
gabbled Oddo, then he threw the pine branch into the stream. It hit the water with a hiss.

'Good,' said Thora, and pointed to the hazel wand. 'Now see if it works!'

Oddo took the wand and began to mark out a circle in the mud of the bank. A spearhead of golden flame shot from the point of the wand and Oddo felt a thrill of excitement.

'It's working!' he yelled.

He turned to look at Thora, hunched on a stone. She was peering intently at the circle scratched in the mud, and he knew she was trying to see the magic fire streaming around it.

Grinning proudly to himself, Oddo squatted in the centre of the ring. He fixed his eyes on the surrounding flames as they grew higher and higher. Was that the shape of an otter on the other side?

He felt himself melting, and pouring across the ground. For a moment he was in the middle of the golden light, and then he was out on the other side, and strength seemed to fill his body again. His muscles tensed, his back arched, and he found himself bounding along the bank.

'I'm an otter!' he thought exultantly. 'I'm an otter!'

To his right, the grasses grew high above his head, but as he leapt, he caught glimpses of the forest beyond. To his left, the bank, looking wide and steep, sloped down to the water. With a whistle of delight he dropped on his belly, tobogganing down the slippery, muddy bank, steeling himself for the shock of diving into freezing water. But he'd forgotten about his waterproof fur! He didn't feel the cold at all.

He swam happily, eyes and nose bobbing above the waterline, front paws curled against his chest. All he had to do to push himself along was wiggle his tail. When he dipped his head into the water, he could feel vibrations through his whiskers. He sensed something swimming close by, and swung round with lightning swiftness to grab a nice fat perch trying to sneak past.

He rolled onto his back with the fish clasped between his paws, and closed his eyes. He savoured the warm sun on his face, the smell of the fish, the feel of the gently rippling water bearing him along . . .

'Oddo! Don't be too long!'

The voice wrenched him out of his pleasant reverie and he glanced towards the shore. A girl was there, peering anxiously at the stream. And a boy, squatting in a ring of fire. Oddo the otter rolled over, swam to the shore, and dropped the fish on the muddy bank.

Thora waited. Beside her, the squatting figure of Oddo stared vacantly, jaw slack, not a muscle moving. Thora avoided looking at it. It made her feel uncomfortable.

'Oddo,' she called impatiently, peering into the water. 'Don't be too long!'

As if in answer, she saw a fish flip out of the river and onto the bank. A moment later it was joined by another.

'Well, how about cooking them, then?' It was Oddo's voice.

Thora swung round in relief. Oddo was grinning at her with his proud, toothy grin. He pointed at the fish.

'I'm starving. I could have eaten them raw!'

Soon the smell of cooking perch rose in the air. Hairydog burst into view on the other side of the stream. She paddled through the water, scrambled out and shook herself dry.

'Trust you to turn up when there's food around,' said Thora.

Thora ate slowly, savouring every bite, watching the play of sunlight on the rippling water. When Oddo spoke, his words ruffled her contentment.

'Why do you think Grimmr's so keen on getting home first?' he asked.

Thora shrugged, threw a fishbone in the water, and wiped her fingers on the grass. 'No idea,' she said.

'There must be a reason,' Oddo persisted.

Thora looked at his fingers wrenching at the reeds. His nervousness flowed through the air like a cold breeze. She picked up a stick and poked at the dying fire.

'I don't see what he can do,' she said.

'He's Grimmr – he could do anything. He could tell the Thingmen I'm not coming. He could burn down our farm. He could steal our animals. He could . . . No!' he grabbed her arm and pointed at the fire. 'It's that!' he cried. '*That's* what Grimmr's planning to do!'

Thora stared at the embers in bewilderment.

'I don't understand.'

'He's going to light a fire on our land! That's all he has to do to stop me! Remember? Erp said – if someone lights a fire on our land before the ceremony starts, I won't be able to get the needfire going! And remember, Grimmr was right behind us, sitting on a horse. He was listening!' He scrambled to his feet, cheeks flushed, eyes glittering. 'Thora, we've got to stop him!'

'We can't,' said Thora. 'He's got a horse! There's no way we can catch up with him, let alone get ahead of him.' She stood too, and began to gather their things.

'Anyway, you said the Little Folk were looking after the farm.'

'What can they do against a big bully like that?!' cried Oddo. 'And they don't know about the needfire and stuff!'

In tense silence, they took off their shoes and waded across the stream. Oddo kept frowning at the path and glancing up at the sun. Eventually, he stopped walking.

'This track's no use – it's veering south and we want to go north!'

'Well, it must be going round a fjord or something,' said Thora. 'Ulf warned us that would happen. It has to twist and bend all over the place.'

'That's crazy. It'll take us forever to get home!'

'I know, but there's nothing we can do about it. We can't make a different path!'

To Thora's astonishment, Oddo whooped with delight. 'That's a brilliant idea. That's exactly what we'll do. We'll make a different path. A short cut!'

'Oh, Oddo, don't be silly. We've got to get round the mountains and forests and things. We . . .'

'No,' said Oddo fiercely. 'We won't go round them. We'll go straight through them!'

He pulled the dagger from his belt and began to hew a way through the brambles and bracken at his feet.

'Oddo, this won't work!'

'Why not? These aren't trees. They're just herbs and stuff. They won't bring me bad luck if I cut them.'

101

He disappeared through the undergrowth. Thora chased after him, trying to dodge the branches that flicked back in her face.

At sunset, they found themselves in a rocky cleft. All around was the sound of running water. Little streamlets trickled down the valley walls.

'What's that roaring noise?' wondered Oddo.

'I bet we're near one of the fjords,' said Thora. The trees parted, and she let out a shout. 'I told you!'

A wide chasm of water blocked their path. It looked as if a giant had thrust his dagger in the land and hewn a gap to let the sea pour in. Cliffs hemmed in the water on all sides, and at the end a waterfall thundered downwards, crashing into the fjord with a foaming roar.

'Now what?' yelled Thora.

Oddo hesitated only a moment. He began to make his way round the narrow shore, stepping carefully from rock to rock. Thora shook her head and followed him. On their left, the deep water, like a vast, rippling mirror, turned the setting sun to liquid fire. On their right, the vertical walls of the cliffs towered over their heads.

As they neared the waterfall, the sound of tumbling water grew so loud they had to yell to make themselves heard. Thora imagined the full force of it pounding down on top of them.

'Oddo!' She leaned towards him. 'How are we supposed to get past the waterfall?'

Oddo jerked his head upwards.

'Climb up and go round the top,' he answered. 'Like that time we went climbing for seabird eggs.'

Thora looked at the hundreds of tiny waterfalls trickling down the surface of the cliff. She slid her hand across the slimy, moss-covered rocks, and shook her head. This was no friendly cliff like the one back home, with easy footholds, and tufts of grass to cling to.

'We can't climb this,' she shouted. 'I knew this wouldn't work. We'll have to turn back and look for that path!'

'Rubbish!'

Oddo threw himself at the cliff and tried to claw his way upwards, but there was nowhere to get a grip on the slippery surface, and he just slithered down again.

He glared at it, panting.

'We'll have to go back,' Thora repeated.

Oddo flopped on the ground and didn't look at her. 'We've only got four days left to get home!' he muttered.

Thora bit her lip. 'And one of those days will be spent going backwards,' she thought, but she didn't say it.

They both turned to look behind them. The rocky coast was barely visible now in the gathering darkness. Neither of them spoke as they curled up on the hard, stony ground to wait for morning.

17
Waterfall

Thora slept fitfully, and even in her dreams she could hear the thunder of the waterfall. When she opened her eyes in the morning, the first thing she saw was its white froth foaming down the cliff face.

'Let's go,' mumbled Oddo. He rose dejectedly to his feet and turned to head back the way they'd come.

'Wait!' Thora was staring intently at the waterfall. Suddenly she grabbed the basket and cauldron and leapt to her feet. 'I think there *is* a way past,' she said.

Tripping and scrambling over the rocks, she reached the torrent of water and squinted her eyes against the spray.

'*Look!*' she called.

Oddo reached her side and peered over her shoulder.

There, behind the tumbling water, they could see a ledge of rock leading to the other side of the fjord.

'We can't walk on that!' said Oddo.

They both stared at the flood of water pouring down the cliff face and crashing over the rocks.

'Do you want to catch up with Grimmr or not?' demanded Thora.

Holding her breath, she stepped onto the ledge. It trembled with the violence of the waterfall, but the water shot over her head in a thundering curtain, and here behind it, she could feel only a fine shower of spray. It felt like a cave made of water. Carefully, she began to shuffle forward. One step . . . two steps . . . Suddenly, her foot slipped. She shrieked, twisted to regain her balance, and let go of the cauldron. It somersaulted through the pounding water. Thora stared in horror as it bumped down over the rocks and disappeared. She gulped.

'That's what'll happen if *I* fall!' she thought.

She pressed her face against the cliff and felt the pulse in her temple beating against the rock. Drops trickled down her face and she realised the fine spray of water was slowly drenching her hair and clothes. She could smell the waterfall – the wet earth and the slimy rocks.

'I don't want to move,' she thought. 'I don't want to take another step.'

'Thora!'

Awkwardly, she twisted her head to look. Oddo was beside her, his eyes black and frightened. And just behind him she could see Hairydog, her paws scrabbling for a grip on the rocks. Thora forced herself to smile.

'I was just waiting for you,' she yelled.

Somehow, she would have to make her legs move again. Biting hard on her lip, she slid one foot along the ledge. She paused and took a shuddering breath. Now for the other foot. Bit by bit she began to edge forward.

'Don't slip!' she kept telling herself. 'And don't drop the basket!' She gripped the handle tight, conscious of the precious silver inside it.

Oddo was so close behind that she could feel his quick, panting breaths. Every now and then his toes butted her heels. She wanted to scream at him to move back. Her own feet seemed huge and clumsy. She kept her eyes fixed on that slippery, narrow track. She kept seeing that cauldron twisting, bouncing down the waterfall, hitting the rocks and vanishing into the foam. The tunnel of grey rock and pounding water seemed to go on forever. Her hands were so numb they couldn't grip properly any more. She was terrified she was going to drop the basket, or lose her hold on the cliff.

Suddenly, Oddo gave a hoot.

'We've done it!' he cried.

Thora had one glimpse of sunlight sparkling through the spray, before an excited Oddo cannoned into her back and sent her toppling forward. Tears of pain and shock sprang to her eyes, but there were dry rocks under her hands and warm sun on her back, and she began to laugh with relief. She lay where she'd fallen and listened to the waterfall thundering downwards – safely behind her. Then she sat up, wiped her stinging palms along her skirt, and turned to look.

'We did it!' she whispered.

She gazed with awe at the pouring water – and the far side of the fjord. She felt weak and shaky, but Oddo was dancing with impatience.

'Come on!' he called.

Reluctantly, Thora staggered to her feet.

A few minutes later, they found themselves on a track again.

'Good!' said Thora, 'I've had enough of shortcuts!'

There was a sound of hoofbeats behind them, and a rider yelled at them to get out of his way.

Thora threw a startled glance at Oddo as they both turned.

It was Grimmr.

The flabbergasted look on his face when he caught sight of them made Thora giggle.

'What the– How did– Where did you pop up from?!' spluttered Grimmr. Then the old familiar roar was back again. 'You'd better watch out!' he warned. 'Get in my way and I'll squash you like a pair of mosquitoes!'

He whipped up his horse and charged towards them. A flying hoof caught Thora on the shoulder as she leapt out of the way. She sprawled, stunned, then sat up, rubbing at her bruise.

'Crotchety crows!' she exclaimed. She stared after him. He was still bellowing at the top of his voice as he rode off. A bow was slung across his back and his belt bristled with weapons.

Oddo grinned.

'Gave him a bit of a surprise, hey?'

'He was *furious*!' said Thora.

'Yeah, well, it's going to muck up his plans when we get home before him, isn't it?'

'But we won't! He's got in front of us again.' Thora glanced at Oddo and her heart sank. 'Not another shortcut!'

Oddo was studying the track. 'Yes,' he agreed, 'We've got to get away from these fjords. If we leave the coast, travel inland, and *then* turn north . . .'

'But . . . there's no path heading inland!' wailed Thora.

Oddo grinned and drew out his dagger. 'We'll soon fix that!' he said.

18
Stuck in a swamp

To Oddo's relief, the forest soon thinned. A few spindly pines were scattered among tufts of heather, low clumps of bilberries and occasional juniper bushes.

'Hey, this is easy!' cried Oddo. He hurdled a bilberry plant and whirled his dagger arm through the air. 'What a brilliant shortcut!'

He turned to grin at Thora. She smiled back, the sunlight bright on her face. From overhead came the sound of many wingbeats. Hairydog barked excitedly. Oddo tilted back his head and watched with awe as a flock of cranes – hundreds and hundreds of them – glided over, trumpeting a greeting. As they flew low above him, their wings, like widespread cloaks, blocked out the sky.

Oddo watched their progress as they sank lower and lower, finally landing in the distance.

'There must be a lake over there,' said Thora.

Their route lay in the same direction as the cranes, and as they drew closer Oddo could see glints of water between the mass of feathered bodies.

He sang as he walked, covering the ground with long, easy strides. Thora kept in step beside him, twirling a stalk and joining in the song.

Suddenly she gave a yell, and stopped.

At the same moment, Oddo felt his foot plunge into something cold and wet.

'Yuck!'

They'd walked straight into a mossy bog. Oddo took another step. The mire sucked and gurgled. The moss sank downwards and water oozed up over his ankles.

Hairydog sniffed at it with interest, then danced off ahead of them, her paws sending up little splashes of water.

Oddo tried to follow, but his feet sank and slithered in the mud. He stopped trying to walk, and stared at the ground ahead. Moss spread before him as far as he could see, like a furry pelt of green, grey and brown, broken here and there by the longer hairs of sedge grass.

'You don't think that's all bog, do you?' he asked.

'It couldn't be,' said Thora.

But with every step the solid-looking ground kept

sinking beneath their feet. Their faces grew glummer and glummer.

'We'll never beat Grimmr at this rate,' moaned Oddo.

On the shore of the lake the cranes were busy prodding for grubs and frogs among the sedges. As Oddo and Thora waded into sight, they raised their beaks and eyed the intruders with curious beady eyes. The surface of the water exploded upwards as hundreds of pink-footed geese rose in a noisy, splashing melee.

'Hey,' called Oddo, and held out his hand.

The geese swirled overhead, then turned back to the lake, skimming the surface and landing again. Oddo waited hopefully. One big gander honked loudly, dived under the water, then paddled towards him. Oddo reached out eagerly and a squirming silver fish was dropped into the palm of his hand.

'Thank you!' he called.

Proudly he displayed his trophy to Thora.

'And just how are we supposed to cook it?' she demanded.

'Uuh . . .' Oddo surveyed the waterlogged ground. Not the perfect place to light a fire. 'We'll just have to eat it raw,' he said.

Thora gulped down her share, then squatted next to a plant with round red leaves. 'Hey, a sundew! Come and look at this!'

Oddo squelched up beside her.

'What am I looking at?' he asked.

'Wait and you'll see.'

They waited without speaking. There was the *plop* of a frog nearby. A little black insect hummed in front of them, drawn by the drops of moisture glinting on the sundew leaves.

'Watch,' breathed Thora.

The insect landed. Tiny wings whirred frantically.

'It can't get off again!' said Oddo, puzzled.

'No,' said Thora. 'It's trapped! That shiny stuff on the leaf is sticky.'

The leaf began to curl around and in a few moments the insect had disappeared inside it. Oddo stared.

'Come on,' said Thora, standing up.

'But . . . what's going to happen now?'

'The sundew will eat the fly.'

'*What?* Plants don't eat insects.'

'This one does!'

As they set off again, Oddo clenched his fists and willed his legs to work harder. But the faster he tried to walk, the more the mire seemed to cling. Would this bog *never* end? He was beginning to feel like an insect himself, with legs trapped in a sticky dew. He imagined his body sinking, and the feathery moss closing over his head, like the sundew leaf around the helpless fly.

'If I don't get out of this soon,' he thought, 'it won't

matter what Grimmr does. I won't be home in time to light the needfire anyway!'

A stain of gold was spreading across the lake. It looked as if the sun was melting into the water. Oddo stared at it in dismay.

'Sunset!' he wailed. 'We've been in this bog all day!'

He looked at Thora, hoping for reassurance, but her eyes reflected his own fears.

By the time they'd passed the lake, daylight was giving way to the shadows of evening. Oddo's legs were so tired he could hardly lift them.

'In a minute, I'll have to call a halt,' he thought.

The next step, his foot slammed against something hard, jarring his whole body. Instead of sinking into a pool, he was standing on solid earth. Hardly daring to believe it, he scanned ahead. In the twilight he could just make out a hint of rising ground and the shapes of trees. Had they reached the end of the bog – at last? Tentatively, he took another step. His wet shoes made a squishing noise, but the ground didn't move.

A few minutes later the two friends were flopped down in front of a campfire. Hairydog writhed on her back, trying to get rid of the mud spattered all over her. Thora spread out her drenched skirt. Steam rose from the wet cloth, filling the air with the odour of warm, peaty water. Oddo yanked off his sodden shoes and grimaced at his feet, white and wrinkled from their long soaking. He lolled back, enjoying the feeling of lying on hard, dry rocks, and closed his eyes.

The next thing he knew, Hairydog's smelly, matted fur was tickling his face. Oddo pushed the dog away and opened his eyes. In the clear morning light he could see the bog stretching endlessly behind him. And in front . . . He stared in disbelief. In front, the ground climbed upwards, steeply, relentlessly, to the peak of a snow-capped mountain! He groaned out loud. How on earth were they going to get past that?

Miserably, he clambered to his feet. Lumps of dried mud cascaded off his breeches. One of them bounced on Thora's face. She blinked and sat up. Her hair hung like strands of rope and her kirtle was patterned with peat-coloured streaks. He watched apprehensively as she took in the sight of the mountain and the snow. To his astonishment, she snorted with laughter.

'I don't believe it,' she said. 'A fjord, a bog, and now – a mountain! You certainly pick them!' She stood up and shook out her skirt. 'Well, we'd better get a move on, hadn't we?'

19

Over the mountains

On the lower slopes there were scattered bushes, birches and pine trees. One of the bushes was loaded with berries – some hard and green, others black and juicy. Oddo plucked a few ripe ones and popped them onto his tongue. He heard Thora's yelp of warning just as he closed his mouth.

'Yuck!'

He spat repeatedly, berries spraying from his mouth, as he tried to get rid of the bitter taste. Thora doubled up, laughing.

'You can't eat juniper berries raw!' she gurgled. 'Here.' She picked a sorrel leaf and held it out to him. 'Eat this instead.'

Oddo eyed the leaf dubiously. It was full of holes and

there was a caterpillar on it. He wondered if he was supposed to eat the caterpillar too. Deciding not, he flicked it off with his finger, and took a tentative bite. It was fresh and tangy and cleaned away the taste of the berries.

As they moved onto higher ground, the bushes thinned. Oddo and Thora walked briskly. At midday, they reached the tree-line. Oddo stepped from the shelter of the last few shrubs and felt a blast of icy wind blowing from the snow above. He lifted his face to the sky.

'Give us a bit more sunshine!' he called.

The slope was steeper now and they had to scramble, half crawling, across the bare rocks.

But the snow, when they reached it, was soft and slushy. Oddo realised too late that the sunshine he'd asked for was making it melt. He sank in right up to his knees.

'You and your shortcuts!' growled Thora, floundering beside him.

Oddo ploughed doggedly onwards. His hands and toes grew so numb he couldn't feel them. After a few minutes he realised Thora was missing. He turned round to find her ripping the branches off a lone birch tree. By the time he'd struggled to her side to see what she was up to, she'd bent one branch into the shape of a fish and was weaving thin, pliable twigs across it.

'Snow shoes!' gasped Oddo. 'Good idea!'

Soon the wide, flat snowshoes were ready for tying on their feet.

'This is better!' cried Oddo. 'I'm not sinking any more!'

Now the ground rose even steeper, and large chunks of snow kept breaking away. Suddenly, Oddo found himself treading on air, and the next moment he was rolling and bouncing down the mountain. He crashed into a tree and came to a jarring halt, the breath knocked from his body.

Spreadeagled on the ground, feeling like a fool, he glared with frustration at the slope he'd have to climb all over again.

Then, as he clambered to his feet, he discovered that his snowshoes had been torn to pieces. Soon he was threshing around helplessly in the slushy snow again. He spied a reindeer watching him, a supercilious expression on its face, and he had a flash of inspiration.

'Hey, you,' he called, 'don't just stand there gawking at me. How about you come here and make yourself useful!'

The reindeer minced towards him on its long, elegant legs. Oddo grabbed an antler and hoisted himself onto its back.

'Go on!' he yelled, kicking his heels. 'Get me out of here!'

The reindeer twisted its head around and nuzzled curiously at Oddo's knee.

'Go *on*,' urged Oddo.

Thora was watching from above.

'You're crazy!' she called. 'That's not a horse!'

Oddo gripped the antlers tight, leaned towards the creature's ear, and spoke as sternly as he could. 'Reindeer,' he said, 'you are going to take me to the top of this mountain!'

The beast took off and they sped up the slope, Oddo bouncing around as helpless as a bag of oats. From the corner of his eye, he spied a younger reindeer galloping beside him, and Hairydog racing to join them.

'Wait!' cried Oddo.

As his mount slowed to a standstill, Oddo gestured to the smaller deer.

'Come here,' he coaxed.

The animal regarded him, head on one side. Then, as if against its will, it edged towards him.

'Thora, this one's for you,' said Oddo. He reached out and placed a hand on the reindeer's neck. He could feel it trembling.

'Sssh,' he soothed.

As Thora sidled closer, he murmured a chant in its ear:

Just for once please kindly lend
Your strong back to help a friend.'

It rolled its eyes but stood still as Thora clambered on.

'Hold tight!' warned Oddo.

The two reindeers tossed their heads and an instant later they were thundering up the mountainside. Snow splattered from their pounding hooves. Hairydog capered and yelped with excitement. A pair of white-plumed willow grouse, invisible against the snow, scattered out of the way, scolding indignantly. Thora and Oddo whooped at the top of their voices.

At the crest of the mountain, the reindeers paused, hot breath steaming from their nostrils, black hooves planted in the sparkling snow. Through the cloth of his breeches Oddo could feel heat and sweat and the heaving of his reindeer's strong, muscly chest.

'I feel like I've been thrashed with a stick!' panted Oddo, rolling his shoulders to relax his own tense muscles. 'There must be bruises all down my legs!'

With one hand he let go of the antlers to massage his bottom. He could hear Thora panting beside him.

Below them the mountain fell away in a steep ravine, then rose again in another snow-capped peak. Without warning, Oddo's steed gave a little skip, and plunged down the slope. Oddo threw his arms round the creature's neck, lurching from side to side, as the reindeer leapt and slithered.

The valley sped towards them. Snow was giving way to the green of foliage. Now they were galloping into trees and overhanging branches, branches that scraped their legs and ripped at their hair. Oddo ducked and caught a glint of water at the bottom of the valley.

'Help!' he thought. 'A river!'

From the corner of his eye he saw Thora and her mount race out in front. Thora's hair and cloak were flying like flags on a mast. The water lay before them, wide, swirling and deep.

'No!' wailed Thora. 'Make it sto-o-op!'

But even as she spoke, her reindeer bounded in. Her last words trailed away and she vanished in a fountain of spray.

Oddo had no time even to shout before his mount, too, was leaping into the river. Icy water swallowed him down, but the next instant he bobbed up again, clinging to the reindeer's back. The river, fed by melting snow, was a surging monster. The reindeer strained forward, neck muscles bulging, and Oddo could feel its legs pumping against the current. Thora, water streaming from her hair and clothes, was hanging onto the neck of her mount and yelling encouragement.

But where was Hairydog? Oddo watched in horror as a speck of nose, a tip of tail flashed into view. The river seemed to be tossing her around like a bit of twig. Maybe, if he threw himself sideways, reached out and grabbed a handful of her fur . . . But then, to his amazement, he realised that the nose and tail were drawing closer to the shore.

Hairydog reached the bank first. As the reindeer scrambled up behind her, Oddo was greeted by a faceful of spray. Hairydog shook herself dry, threw him a grin, then trotted away. Thora's mount took off after her, with Thora squealing and grabbing the antlers to save herself from falling.

Oddo chuckled, but his smile soon froze to a grimace as his own reindeer began to gallop, and the cold wind cut through his wet clothes.

The second mountain seemed to go up and up forever. Oddo's hands grew rigid and numb. Night was falling by the time they reached the crest and started down the other side.

At last they reached the bottom. The reindeers slowed to a stop, and they waited, stamping their feet.

Oddo peeled his hands from the antlers and slithered stiffly to the ground. His legs almost crumpled under him. He patted the reindeers' necks and whispered a thankyou in their ears before they flicked their heels and sped away.

Oddo hobbled around, alternately flapping his arms and rubbing his legs, while Thora flopped at the foot of a tree.

'Hey,' Oddo called. 'How about one of your famous remedies! I'm sore all over.'

'I'm too tired,' Thora mumbled.

She wrapped herself in her cloak, and curled up to sleep.

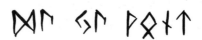

20
Wolf pack

Oddo woke before the dawn. He was shivering and every muscle in his body hurt. He groaned and sat up.

'A warm fire would help,' he thought. Hairydog opened one eye. 'Come on,' Oddo whispered. 'Help me find some firewood. We'll make a surprise for Thora when she wakes up.'

Hairydog leapt to her feet, snuffling with excitement, and quickly disappeared from sight. Moving slowly on his stiff legs, Oddo made his way between the trees.

The forest was dense and dark, with moonlight breaking through in splotches of silver. His feet made soft swishing sounds through the dead leaves, and he jumped when a fallen branch crunched underfoot. He bent to pick it up and snapped it into pieces as he walked. There was a splashing noise, and a wide lake came into view. Hairydog was paddling out from shore, carving a clear wake in its black surface. Sleepy ducks rose out of her way, flapped, and settled again on the water.

When Thora opened her eyes it was still dark. She lay listening to the forest noises, wondering what had woken her. A wind whistled through the branches, making her shiver.

'Brrr, I'm cold.' She pulled her cloak more tightly around her. 'Hey, Oddo, are you awake? Can you make that wind go away?' She rolled over.

Oddo wasn't there.

'Oddo?' She sat up and looked around. A tight fist of fear clutched at her heart. 'Hairydog?' She could hear the sound of panic in her voice.

Where could they be? Why would they go anywhere in the dark? Had something happened to them?

Thora scrambled to her feet, her mind filled with memories of Grimmr's threats.

'Oddo,' she called again, trying to sound brave this time. 'I'm coming to find you. Don't worry, I'm coming!'

It was then she heard the wolves.

The first howl, high and piercing, came from the left. Before the echoes died away there was another, throaty and menacing; then another. And another.

Thora began to run, but all among the trees there were sounds of pattering feet, and suddenly a wolf, ghostly grey-coloured with eyes glowing in the moonlight, was barring her way. Thora whirled round and blundered in another direction. She could feel her heart pounding, her breath coming in gasps. And now there were grey shapes everywhere she looked, flickering in and out of sight.

A branch clawed at her face. She reached up angrily and snapped it off. There was another howl, and a lean wolf, hackles raised, sprang out in front of her. Thora stood still, panting, glaring into its eyes. She lifted the stick and brandished it in the creature's face, but it didn't even flinch. And now there were wolves all round her. She could sense them. They growled and swished their tails, and on every side, she could see the spark of their red eyes gleaming among the shadows.

Thora lifted her stick and brought it down hard on the first wolf's nose. To her dismay, instead of falling back, it reared up with a snarl. Then all the wolves burst out of the trees, leaping and snapping. Thora tried to dodge out of their way, slashing wildly with her stick, but they knocked the weapon from her hands, and then she heard a loud *rrrrip* as sharp teeth closed on her sleeve and yanked.

Oddo was having a difficult time finding sticks in the dark. He peered in the shadows under the trees and scuffed round with his feet. Ah, a big fallen branch. He was bending to pick it up when a howl sounded from the depths of the trees.

He looked up, startled.

Another howl followed, louder, stronger than the one before.

Wolves!

Oddo whirled round and tore into the forest.

The howls were echoing all around him now.

'Thora!' he yelled. 'Thora, I'm coming!'

He was running so fast he felt as if he were flying. He hurtled between the trees, then skidded to a halt, gaping at the scene in front of him.

Thora was surrounded by a pack of wolves, but the beasts seemed frozen in mid-snarl. As Oddo watched, they all fell back and turned their heads in the direction of the dying echoes. They waited, ears pricked, tails raised.

Out of the shadows, walking like a prince, came the stately figure of a huge wolf. Oddo felt his heart beating fast, but Thora just lowered her arm. To Oddo's astonishment, she whispered something to the creature, then knelt down and let the wolf reach forward and touch his muzzle to the tip of her nose.

Oddo couldn't bear it any longer.

'Thora!' he cried. 'What on earth is going on? Since when have you had power over animals?'

Thora swung round in surprise at the sound of his voice, then smirked at him and stood up.

'Don't you recognise him?' she asked. 'It's Grey Wolf – you know, the one we rescued!'

Oddo's jaw dropped. He lowered his gaze, and there, bound round the hind leg, just where Thora had tied it, was the last remaining tatter of a bandage.

'Grey Wolf!' he breathed. 'And I thought you were being eaten!'

'What about you?' demanded Thora. 'Where've you been? I thought Grimmr had kidnapped you or something!'

'I went to find sticks to make a fire, but . . .' He looked at his empty hands. 'I think I dropped them all when I came racing to the rescue.'

Thora raised her eyebrows. 'You were making a fire? In the middle of the night?'

Oddo looked at the streaks of dawn peeping over her shoulder. 'It's not night, it's morning,' he said. 'And it's light enough to see where we're going. Come on, we've only got two days left to get home!'

↑ᚱ ᛒᛁ

21
A warm welcome

'My shoes are all holes, and these brambly things aren't exactly pleasant to walk on,' grumbled Thora, a few hours later.

Oddo slashed angrily at a branch. His shoes were worn out too, and his arm ached from hacking a way through the forest. He ground his teeth at the thought of Grimmr riding in comfort along the pathway.

By the end of the day, even Hairydog was drooping, and dragging her paws.

'I wish I hadn't lost the cauldron,' mourned Thora. 'Hot porridge would have been nice right now.'

'A lot of things would have been nice right now,' thought Oddo. 'A bed, a hot fire . . .'

He took another step and blinked in astonishment.

In front of him, like the answer to a dream, stood a farmhouse. It was perched upon a cliff above the waters of a fjord, lit by the glow of the setting sun. Smoke curled from its green turf roof. Hens pecked in its yard. A cow peered over the low door of the barn, a wisp of hay in its mouth.

'A hot fire!' cried Oddo.

'Food!'

'A bath!'

'A nice soft bed!'

'We shouldn't really stop,' said Oddo. 'We've got to be home by tomorrow. And Grimmr –'

'Oh come on, Grimmr's miles behind us, surely. And we must be nearly home.'

Thora led the way across the yard. There was a roar of angry barking and two guard dogs hurtled round the corner of the house. Hairydog started forward, growling protectively, but Oddo grabbed her by the scruff of the neck and fell to his knees, pulling Thora down beside him.

'We're friends!' he assured the strange dogs.

The dogs stopped their clamour and padded over, noses quivering with curiosity. Oddo, Thora and Hairydog waited to be sniffed and inspected before they rose to their feet again. Then the strange dogs led them, tails wagging, to the front of the house.

At the doorway, Oddo and Thora stopped and looked at each other, puzzled. There were no hangings here of animal skins like the houses at home. This doorway was filled with planks of studded wood, like the side of a clothes chest. And it was framed with carved dragons like the figurehead of a longship.

'How do we get in?' breathed Thora.

Oddo pushed at the wood, hoping it would swing aside like a normal door hanging, but it didn't move.

'Hey!' he called. 'Is anybody home?'

'Maybe we're supposed to bang on it,' suggested Thora. She thumped with her hand.

They heard someone moving inside. There was a scraping noise, and the wooden door swung open.

A squat little woman poked her head around the door.

'Two children!' she cried. 'Didn't Mani and Tanni frighten you, then?'

She frowned at the guard dogs, who were standing and wagging their tails.

Oddo stared back at her in astonishment. It was old Gyda, the midwife who'd brought him into the world.

'Gyda Goodwife!' he cried. 'Don't you recognise us?'

The woman squinted and leaned closer.

'Why, it's Oddo and Thora!' she exclaimed. 'Two of my babies!'

'Can we come in?' asked Thora, stepping forward. 'We're starving, and . . .'

'Goodness, I'm forgetting my manners!' The old midwife pushed the door back. 'Come in! Sit by the fire and toast your toes. I've a nice hot meal just ready to be eaten.'

Indoors was like a cosy nest. On the welcoming hearth in the middle of the room, a pot of oat graut simmered over the flames. Rustling straw softened the hard earth floor, and cushions padded the wooden stools. Instead of one long room, like the houses at home, this one was divided into chambers with panels.

'Is this where you live now?' asked Thora.

Gyda nodded and smiled. Her chins trembled and her coils of hair wobbled.

'Yes, I've moved in with my son and his boys,' she said. 'But they're off on a Viking raid just now.'

She placed a steaming bowl of water on the table. Thora dipped her hands in and reached for the towel. Oddo gazed at the bowl of graut Gyda was filling for him, licking his lips as she added a dollop of sweet, sticky honey.

'Now tell me what you're doing here,' said Gyda, placing it in front of him.

Before Oddo could answer, Thora burst out proudly.

'We've been to the Gula Thing!' she said. 'And now we're heading home. Is it much further?'

'Ooh no, just a few hours away. Follow the path along this fjord and you'll find a river that leads straight to your house.'

Oddo banged his spoon and gave a hoot of triumph.

'We've done it!' he cried.

'I told you,' said Thora.

'Now, you just hurry and get your bellies filled,' said Gyda. 'And get out of these daggled clothes.' She pinched the wet cloth of Oddo's cloak. 'It's the bath-house you'll visit next, and then bed.'

22

Unpleasant surprise

Oddo stepped inside the bath-house and felt his last niggling worries melt away. The comforting warmth of the air seeped right through to his bones.

He emptied a bucket of water onto the heated hearth stones, making them sizzle and steam. Sitting down in the thick white vapour, he stretched out his legs and giggled when he couldn't see his toes. With a switch of soft birch twigs, he began to slap his arms and legs. The scent of birch filled the air and his skin tingled. Dirt and sweat oozed out, like the steam rising from the rocks.

He tilted a dipper full of cold water over his head, shivering as it ran down his hot skin. Feeling fresh and clean, he wrapped himself in a warm towel, and padded out to the sleeping chamber.

Gyda was there waiting for him with a bundle in her arms.

'Here.' She shook out a clean linen undershirt, tunic and breeches. 'These belonged to my grandsons when they were younger. But I'm afraid I never had grand-daughters.'

Oddo followed her gaze. Thora, swathed in a kirtle twice her size, was standing in the middle of the room looking very embarrassed. Long, dangling sleeves swallowed up her hands, and the skirt was bunched up round her waist with a rope. Oddo had to hold his breath to stop himself snorting with laughter.

Thora glared at him, then gathered up her trailing garments and tripped across to the sleeping bench.

'What's that?' asked Oddo, pointing at a square of amber that glowed high up in the end wall.

'Why, a window!' cried Gyda.

It was a hole, covered with the thinnest of animal skins.

'That's the setting sun you can see shining through,' she explained.

A few minutes later, Oddo was curled up in bed, with Hairydog at his back.

'Oddo,' said Thora. 'No more shortcuts! Tomorrow we follow the pathway.'

'No more shortcuts,' Oddo chuckled. 'Anyway, if we're so close to home, it wouldn't make a difference!'

Across the room, Gyda the Midwife hesitated in the doorway and slewed round towards them.

'There's something I've got to tell you.' Her voice sounded hoarse. 'Might not be another chance . . . I'm getting old . . .' She took a breath, then seemed to change her mind. 'No,' she muttered. 'The morning will do. I'll tell you in the morning.' She shambled away.

'What was that about?' whispered Thora.

Oddo shrugged.

'It can't be anything important – she's just a funny old woman,' he said, and snuggled into the soft feather mattress. Through the doorway he could see Gyda settling down to mend their cloaks by firelight. He listened to the quiet shifting of logs in the hearth, the steady rhythm of Thora's breathing. Overhead, the orange glimmer in the window darkened to black. Oddo smiled contentedly and closed his eyes. A picture of himself marching in front of a cheering crowd, holding up the needfire, sparkled in his mind. As he drifted off to sleep, he imagined Bolverk's beaming face and all the things he would say in praise of his son.

A thunder of barking split the silence. Oddo and Thora shot up in bed. Fists pounded on the door.

'Call off these jabbering hounds before I take my sword to them!'

'Coming! Patience!' Gyda rose in a fluster. Her mending cascaded to the floor. 'Another traveller?' she queried, drawing back the bolts and peering round the door. 'Down, Tanni. Quiet, Mani.'

'Inhospitable curs!' bawled the stranger, thrusting Gyda aside and stumping into the room. With his bald head, forked beard, and bulging, firelit eyes, he looked like an ogre. But . . .

'Grimmr!' gasped Oddo.

'How did he catch up with us?'

'I told you we shouldn't stay.'

'Puffin poop! Who was it stuffed himself with graut and stayed in the bath for hours?' The two friends glared at each other. 'Anyway, it doesn't matter now. Let's get out of here,' said Thora. 'If we leave and Grimmr stays here, we can still beat him home!' She threw back her cover and swung her feet to the floor.

'But we can't leave!' Oddo exclaimed. 'There's only one door and it's over there.' He pointed into the other room, where Grimmr and Gyda were standing by the doorway.

Thora looked round wildly. She even looked up at the ceiling.

'The window!' she whispered. 'We can get out the window! Quick!' She stood on the bed. 'Get up here and I'll climb on your shoulders. Where's your dagger?'

As Thora clambered onto his back, Oddo struggled to keep his balance. The dagger wavered alarmingly in

Thora's hand, then disappeared from sight as the smothering folds of her kirtle dropped over his eyes. He could feel her jerky movements as she hacked at the window covering.

The next instant, her weight lifted from his shoulders, and there she was, perched on the windowsill, a silhouette framed by the square of moonlight.

Hairydog leapt on the bed, panting eagerly.

'Sssh!' hissed Oddo.

Quickly, he hoisted her up to Thora, then passed up the basket.

He was standing there, arms outstretched, when a voice roared behind him. Oddo spun round. Grimmr was glaring from the doorway, a burning torch in his hand.

'You!' he bellowed. 'What are you up to?!'

'Oddo!' squealed Thora. 'Stop him! Use your magic!'

'Rain and wind, I summon you!' gasped Oddo.

There was a streak of lightning, then a howling gale ripped at his clothes and sent him reeling against the wall. Thunder roared, and rain streamed from the rafters. Grimmr's torch fizzled out, pitching the room into blackness. Gyda shrieked, and Grimmr blundered around, cursing and crashing into furniture.

'Now what do I do?' thought Oddo wildly.

Hallveig's rope came hurtling downwards, slapping him in the face. He grabbed the dangling plait of nettle just as Thora disappeared from sight. The next instant he was flying upwards. His shoulders hit the frame of the window, jammed for a moment, and then he was through, and landing with a crash on the ground.

The moon shone on a still, calm world. Shakily, Oddo stood up and brushed the wet hair from his eyes.

'Well, that was useless!' Thora snorted. 'I told you to *stop* him! All you did was *wet* him! Now what are we supposed to do?'

At that moment, the guard dogs erupted round the corner of the house, baying wildly.

'Find them! Chase those scoundrels!' Grimmr roared from inside.

23
Wolfspell

'Tanni! Mani!' called Oddo. 'Here!'

The two dogs immediately stopped their barking and pattered towards him.

'Good dogs,' said Oddo.

Grimmr burst out of the house, yelling in fury.

'Now what?' said Thora.

Oddo flashed her a mischievous grin, then raised his eyes to the sky. He muttered something she couldn't hear and instantly, a bank of dense black clouds streamed across the moon. The farm was plunged into darkness.

'Children, children, be careful!' Gyda was calling now, her voice anxious. 'Don't you go running in the dark.'

'Mani!' Thora could hear the excitement in Oddo's voice even though he was whispering. 'Go to the edge of the cliff. Stand there and bark. Make them think we've fallen over. And . . . here!' He grabbed the dog just as it was running off. 'Take this and drop it on the ground to lead them there.'

'What are you giving him?' whispered Thora.

'My pouch. Now . . . Tanni! You go back to Gyda and pretend you're frantic. Take her to the edge of the cliff with you. Go on!'

Panting with eagerness, the dogs scampered away. The moon sneaked out from behind a cloud, revealing the shadowy farmyard and the two shouting figures. Oddo ducked behind the woodpile and Thora hunkered down beside him.

'Hadn't we better go?' she asked.

'Ssshh – in a minute!'

Oddo peered over the logs, and Thora, following his gaze, saw Gyda stop at the edge of the cliff.

'A rope!' cried the old woman, and she hobbled towards the house. The worry lines on her face were deep, black furrows.

'Oh, Oddo,' whispered Thora, 'I feel so mean. She was really kind to us and now we've upset her!'

But Oddo's expression was gleeful.

'Don't fuss,' he said. 'As soon as the sun comes up, she'll find out her mistake. But while Grimmr thinks we're down there, we've got a few hours to get ahead.

That's what you wanted, isn't it? Come on!' He straightened up. 'Let's go!'

They set off through the darkness. Under her bare soles, Thora felt the worn cobblestones of the farmyard give way to the painful, sharp pebbles of the pathway. The hem of her long, wet skirt kept tangling round her feet.

'Don't let me really fall down the cliff!' she prayed.

Frantically, she scooped up armfuls of her kirtle, to keep the trailing hem from tripping her, and hurried to keep up.

Oddo ran as if he'd never stop. Thora staggered along behind, trying to ignore the pain in her side, the ache in her arms, and the numbness of her feet.

With the first sign of dawn came the shriek of gulls and gannets, wheeling and diving for their breakfast. Their nests were piled, tier upon tier, on the rocky cliff that tumbled from the pathway to the fjord.

At last, to Thora's relief, Oddo stopped running. She stumbled to a halt, dropped the wet folds of her kirtle and stretched her stiff arms.

'Give me your dagger,' she panted, 'and I'll cut this blasted thing shorter.' She hacked at the hem of her skirt, then bound the spare strips of damp cloth round her feet. 'All right, I'm ready again!'

To her surprise, Oddo didn't move.

'I thought we'd be home by now,' he said, 'and we haven't even found the river yet!'

'It could be just round the corner,' she said hopefully. 'With all those trees and windy bits we wouldn't know.'

'But even if it is, we're still hours from home. Stupid old Gyda, why did she say it was close when it isn't?'

'I think she just said what we wanted to hear,' said Thora. 'She likes to make people happy. But I reckon she was going to tell us the truth in the morning. Remember – she hinted something last night. The only problem was . . .' She lifted her chin and grinned cockily. 'We scudded off before she could tell us!'

Oddo frowned at her.

'Well, a fat lot of good that did! Now we're nowhere near home. And any second, Grimmr's going to work out we tricked him and come galloping after us!'

'Well, he's not here yet!' Thora declared. 'Come on, let's hurry!'

But instead of running, Oddo scuffed at the ground.

Thora was horrified. 'Hey.' She took his hand and tried to jolly him along. '*You're* not the sort of person to give up!'

Oddo didn't answer.

'Come on!' Thora exclaimed. 'When Grimmr gets here, we'll just do something to slow him down. Trip up his horse or . . . Yes, that's it!' She tugged Oddo round to face her. 'We can frighten the horse, make it run away . . .'

Oddo didn't lift his head.

'How?' he growled.

Thora racked her brain for ideas.

'I know! You can ask Grey Wolf to bring his wolf pack here. That'll work! The wolves will scare the horse and then it will rear up and throw Grimmr off, and it will run away and then Grimmr won't be able to beat us any more!'

She gabbled on, watching Oddo turn over her idea in his mind.

'Maybe . . .' he said consideringly. But then, to her intense disappointment, he shook his head. 'No, it wouldn't be fair to the wolves. Grimmr's got that bow and arrow and stuff. He'd kill them!'

Thora stared at him in frustration.

'Then . . .' Inspiration struck. 'Then make some *magic* wolves!' she burst out triumphantly. 'My brother Erik can magic up animals, and you're much better at spells than he is!'

She held her breath. This time, Oddo didn't shake his head.

'How does he do it?' he asked cautiously.

'He uses leaves and sticks . . .'

'Leaves and sticks! We've got plenty of those!' Oddo gestured at the trees and bushes. 'What animals does he make?' His eyes were brightening with enthusiasm.

'Uh, butterflies, rats . . .' Oddo waited. She shrugged. 'That's all, I think.'

Oddo pulled a face.

'So he doesn't make big animals like wolves?'

'No, but *you* could. Look.' She swept up a fistful of leaves and twigs. 'He makes a butterfly like this.' She laid a twig on the ground, with leaves on either side for wings. 'Now, here. You try.' Excitedly, she dipped into the basket, drew out the hazel wand and handed it to him. 'Go on.'

Doubtfully, Oddo took the wand and tapped the butterfly shape.

Nothing happened.

'Am I supposed to say a spell or something?' he asked.

Thora chewed her lip and looked at him anxiously.

'I don't know.'

Oddo snorted and stood up.

'We're just wasting time,' he said. He threw the wand on the ground and stumped off down the path.

'Oddo, wait!' called Thora, scrambling to her feet and piling the wand back into the basket. 'Quick, Hairydog, come on.'

Oddo was striding now, a furious scowl on his face. He disappeared among the trees.

A minute later, Thora heard a yell. When she rounded the bend, Oddo and Hairydog were standing stock still, staring at a river gushing across their path.

'The river!' cried Thora. 'We're nearly home!' She grabbed Oddo's arm. 'You *can't* let Grimmr get past us now. You've got to do that wolfspell!'

'And I tell you, I can't,' growled Oddo.

'You've hardly tried,' said Thora. 'Maybe you need to use different plants or something.'

'You and your herbs!' snapped Oddo. 'I'm not trying to cure a cough or a sore leg!'

'No, I mean plants that help magic things happen! You know, like the flowers we put in the circle when you make a wand.'

Oddo tilted his head to one side and she saw a glint of interest in his eyes.

'What plants?' he demanded.

Thora rubbed her forehead, trying to remember the plants her family used for spells.

'Well, hazel of course, like your wand. And yarrow, dandelion, mugwort, marigold, wormwood . . . Look, I'll find you some.'

She darted among the trees, snatching up twigs and leaves, then hurried back and poured them on the ground at Oddo's feet.

'Here!' she said, sorting through the jumble of foliage. 'These are hazel twigs. They're for protection.'

Oddo squatted down beside her.

'That sounds right! And these pointy leaves? What are they? They look a bit like teeth. Or ears.'

'Dandelion leaves. They're good for all sorts of magic. And so's this one, yarrow – and look, it's like a bushy tail.' Thora brushed her hand across the feathery foliage.

She could feel Oddo beginning to prickle with

excitement. She picked up another leaf and held it out to him. 'Mugwort – that's supposed to bring strength . . . And *these*!' She pounced on some furry fingers of moss and brandished them proudly. 'They're called wolf's foot!'

Oddo leaned forward as she began to arrange the collection in front of him. Finally, she sat back and looked at him for approval.

There, lying on the ground, was a wolf made of leaves, moss and hazel twigs.

'It *looks* good,' said Oddo, 'but . . .'

Hairydog growled and turned to face the path.

'Grimmr's coming!' Thora's voice squeaked with agitation. 'Go on,' she urged. 'You can do it!'

Oddo stared at the leaves, not speaking. Into the waiting silence came the faint thud of distant hoofbeats.

'*Hurry!*' begged Thora.

Oddo took a breath. He began to chant and his eyes seemed to sparkle with fire:

Where only leaf or twig now lies
Make a living wolf arise!'

Thora clenched her fists. The leaves were quivering, but was it just the wind? The hoofbeats were getting louder, closer.

'Come on,' Thora pleaded. 'You've got to work.'

Her eyes were blurring from staring so hard. The leaves and twigs seemed to be dissolving in a haze of

145

green and brown – no, not green and brown, grey and white. She rubbed her eyes, then opened them again, and cried out in excitement.

'Yes!'

A wolf was stumbling to its feet. It moved stiffly, and its ears were rather large, but when it opened its mouth it showed a perfect set of sharp white teeth.

Oddo was goggling at it in astonishment.

'I did it!' he whispered. 'I made a wolfspell!'

Hairydog was yipping urgently. Thora glanced over her shoulder and caught a glimpse of Grimmr galloping round a bend in the path. Frantically, she snatched up leaves and twigs and piled them haphazardly into wolf shapes.

'Come on,' she yelled. 'Make more! One's not enough!'

ᚦᛖᚾ ᛏᚱᛋ

24
Disaster

The horse was in full view now, pounding towards them, with Grimmr standing in the stirrups hollering and waving his whip.

Every muscle in Thora's body screamed at her to jump out of the way, but Oddo was chanting his spell, his eyes blazing as he pointed at a heap of leaves.

The ground vibrated under the horse's thudding hooves.

Another wolf rose from the leaves, tail lashing, and Oddo raised his hand again. But Thora felt the wind of Grimmr's whip. She saw the horse's glossy, sweat-soaked body, the flaring nostrils.

'Jump!' she cried.

She threw herself sideways – just as the horse skidded to a halt, neighing in terror.

Grimmr soared through the air, his arrows flying from their quiver. He rolled over, then staggered to his feet, spluttering with rage, and drew his sword with a loud *scrrrape*.

The magic wolves milled around him, slavering and snarling, and he reached out to slash at them with his sword. The shock on his face as the blade just sliced through the pack made Thora hoot with glee. One wolf sank its teeth into Grimmr's leg and began to pull.

'Hey!' yelled Grimmr, swinging wildly with his sword.

The wolf let go and Grimmr toppled backwards with a roar. As he tried to beat off the claws tearing and scratching at him, Oddo gave a shout, and pointed.

'Look!' he cried.

Grimmr's horse was galloping into the distance.

'Yes!' yelled Thora. 'We did it!'

Grimmr staggered to his feet, eyes bloodshot, clothes in tatters. He threw Thora a look of hatred.

'You witch!' he croaked.

He tried to run, but a large wolf blocked his way, growling and baring its teeth.

'All right, Wolf, that's enough!' called Oddo.

He stepped forward to pull the creature away, and Grimmr lifted his sword for one last swipe . . .

'No!' screamed Thora, as the sword blade fell.

But Grimmr, free at last, hastened away without even glancing over his shoulder.

Behind him, Oddo crumpled to the ground, and a bright thread of red began to trickle across the pathway.

'Oddo!'

Thora rushed towards him, all her laughter and elation drained away. The face that turned to hers was as white as the feathers of a willow grouse, but the cloth of his breeches was red with blood.

Oddo tried to smile.

'Time for Thora's healing tricks!' he whispered. 'You'd better be quick. I've got to catch up with Grimmr!'

'But I don't have a cauldron for boiling a potion!' wailed Thora.

She pressed her fingers to her temples and tried to think. What herbs could she use that didn't need to be boiled?

'Yarrow!' she cried, 'The leaves will staunch the blood. And chickweed . . .'

Frantically she thrust bushes aside, heedless of the spikes of brambles and the prick of nettles, searching for the plants she needed.

And then she stopped and stared. At her feet was the single furry stem of a mountain sun bloom. Never yet had she dared to use that smelly flower with its pungent taste and knobbly roots. 'Just you be careful with that one,' Granny had warned her. 'It may do your patients the world of good, but it can also kill them!' Thora grabbed a stick, thrust it under the roots and levered the sun bloom out of the ground.

A few moments later, she was back by Oddo's side. As she picked up his dagger, his eyes widened.

'I've just . . . got to . . . get at your leg,' she said, trying to hack at the blood-drenched cloth of his breeches.

She wrapped the wound in yarrow leaves and chick-weed, tying them tightly in place with cloth torn from her kirtle. She rolled a rock under Oddo's leg to raise it off the ground. Then she sat back on her heels to watch.

The bleeding stopped; but Oddo's lips were now as white as his face, and he hardly seemed to be breath-ing. Thora touched his hand, and his skin felt cold.

She looked at the sun bloom lying on the ground beside her, the soil still clinging to its dark, ugly roots.

'I'm going to make an infusion,' she announced, picking up the flower. 'I just need some water to soak this in.' She rummaged in her basket. 'My leather pouch will do for a water bag.'

Impatiently, she upended the basket and shook out the contents. Out fell a stone, the bag of barley and the braided rope.

But no pouch.

Feverishly, Thora scrabbled through the jumble again. She could feel her heart thudding and she knew her cheeks were turning as pink as Oddo's were white. She glanced up and saw Oddo's eyes half open, watching her.

'What's . . . the matter?' he stammered.

'My pouch of silver,' cried Thora. 'It's gone!'

ᚦᛁᛋ ᚱᛗᚾ...

25
Oddo returns

Oddo's eyes widened and they stared at each other in disbelief.

Thora pictured her family waiting at home, trusting her to bring home the taxes. Then she stood up and blotted it out of her mind.

'Never mind,' she said, 'I'll find something different to carry the water in . . .'

She spied a loose strand of bark hanging off a tree. In an instant, she had ripped it off, coiled it into the shape of a drinking horn and was racing down to the river.

'Stay there, Hairydog,' she called. 'And keep Oddo warm!'

A moment later she was back, but one glance at Oddo's blanched face and closed eyes set her frantically crumbling the sun-bloom root and tearing petals from its bud. She dropped them into her improvised cup, then sat back on her heels, forcing herself to wait till the healing powers of the plant had seeped into the water.

Propping up Oddo's head, she lowered the cup to his lips. To her exasperation, most of the infusion trickled down his chin. Impetuously, she dipped a corner of her sleeve into the liquid, and pressed the dripping cloth between his lips. Almost immediately, colour returned to his cheeks, his eyelids flickered, and he opened his eyes.

'Augh!' he said, spitting out the cloth. 'What's this disgusting stuff you're feeding me?'

Thora smiled as tears of relief rolled down her cheeks.

'It's a healing herb,' she said. 'Just have a little bit more.'

Oddo pushed away Thora's hand and scrambled to his feet. For a moment, everything swayed, and he clutched a tree branch to steady himself. Then his head cleared, and there was Thora standing in front of him, arms crossed, and scowling.

'We've got to hurry!' Oddo exclaimed. He set off at a fast hobble, then realised Thora wasn't following. He swung round, agitated. 'Come on. If we run, I can get home in time to stop Grimmr!'

But as he saw her shake her head, he remembered the missing silver.

'Oddo.' Her voice was hoarse. 'I've got to go back. I've got to find the pouch.'

Oddo clenched his fists in panic.

'No!' he cried. 'I have to get home. I *have* to.'

The words screamed in his head. If he wanted to save the farm he had to go right *now*!

'And I have to go back,' said Thora quietly.

Oddo stared at her in despair.

'But . . . I can't go back!' he wailed.

'I know,' said Thora. 'It's all right. Don't worry. You go home. I can manage on my own. It can't be very far. I must have lost my pouch when we climbed out that window.'

'But that's a full day's walk away!' cried Oddo.

He didn't know what to do. If he turned back with Thora he'd give up all hope of saving the farm, but if he went on, he'd be abandoning his friend.

He gazed at her in agony.

'I'll be fine,' said Thora. 'Really. Look.' She opened her fist and showed him a runestone. 'I found this in my basket. It's a good-luck rune Father made for you, to help at the Thing. I never got the chance to give it to you, and then I forgot about it , . . Anyway, if you let me take Hairydog, I'm sure she'll look after me.' She smiled down at the dog.

'Yes,' said Oddo, pouncing on the idea. 'She can help

154

you find the pouch! And here.' He pulled the dagger from his belt. 'Take this.'

'Don't be silly. I won't need it.'

Oddo glared. He limped forward and pushed it into her hand. 'I can't let you go alone if you don't take it,' he said.

Thora pursed her lips and looked down at his leg.

'Oh, all right. Now, get home as fast as you can,' she ordered. 'And remember, no lighting fires! Stay at my house tonight.'

'But your family!' Oddo exclaimed. 'What will they say when I turn up without you?'

'Just tell them I wanted to do something more, and I'll be home soon.'

'I could send one of your brothers to help you . . .'

'No!' cried Thora fiercely. 'I don't want them thinking I can't manage. This is the first time they've depended on me instead of on their magic, and I'm not going to fail them!'

Oddo bounded down the track, ignoring his sore leg. Out of the corner of his eye he caught sight of familiar landmarks flashing past: neighbouring farms, a broken boat, a lonely old elm tree. But where was Grimmr?

'I've been too slow!' thought Oddo in panic. 'He's going to beat me!'

He forced himself to run faster. He was almost

tripping with every step. His leg was burning. At last, on the other side of the river, the fields that led to his own home came into view. He stopped, and gazed up at the bare earth. In a few weeks he'd be toiling those slopes, weeding and planting.

Or would he? Maybe they'd belong to Grimmr!

'No!' he exclaimed. 'That ogre isn't going to win. He *can't* be far ahead of me. He can't have lit a fire yet!'

Ulf's wife was washing clothes on the river bank. At the sound of Oddo's voice, she looked up and beamed a welcome.

'I'll come and fetch you,' she called. She untied a boat drawn up among the reeds and rowed towards him.

'Is Grimmr back?' asked Oddo anxiously, as he hopped on board.

'Hmmph, that he is. More's the pity.'

Oddo's heart sank. He sprang out of the boat almost before it reached the bank, and with a breathless 'Thank you', set off up the slope.

As he ran, his eyes raked the fields for any sign of trouble. He crested the hill, heart thudding wildly, but the sight of his home standing as he'd left it, with no wisp of grey rising from the smoke-hole, brought a sigh of relief.

Then he noticed a goat standing on the roof of the barn tugging at the turf. Another goat was scratching its back against the wall, and another . . . Oddo looked round in astonishment. There seemed to be goats everywhere!

'But we don't own any goats,' he thought, puzzled. 'Where did they come from?'

Scratching his head, he moved towards the barn.

Just before the entrance, he stopped and drew a breath. What was he going to find inside? Would the cows and sheep be all right? With his heart in his mouth, he took another step and peered over the low door.

Two healthy cows glanced up from their contented chewing and lowed a greeting. The sheep scrambled to their feet and rushed towards him, jostling and bleating. With a huge grin, Oddo reached over and rubbed the nearest curly head. He took in the brimming feed troughs, the floor swept clean of dung, the glossy coats of the cows, and the fluffy, combed fleeces of the sheep.

'Thank you, Little Folk,' he breathed. 'Thank you.'

Footsteps thudded on the cobblestones behind him.

Oddo spun round.

'You conniving, cheating cowpat!'

Grimmr was pounding across the yard, brandishing a long stick and bellowing in anger.

↑

26
Willow-bark brew

'You cheat!' repeated Grimmr. 'You measly maggot!'
He reached Oddo, and shook the stick under his nose.
'Thought you'd get away with it, hey? Thought I
wouldn't know it was you opened my barn door and
let out my goats?'

He thrust his boggling eyes in Oddo's face, then
turned and chased after his livestock.

Oddo leaned against the barn wall, shaking. But at
the sight of Grimmr galumphing round the fields, goats
skittering away from him in all directions, he began
to chuckle with relief.

'Grimmr can't go lighting fires and spoiling my
ceremony while he's chasing his precious goats!'

He turned back to the barn and peered around,

hoping to catch sight of one of the Little Folk.

'Was that your doing?' he whispered. 'Did *you* let Grimmr's goats out?'

As usual, there was no answer.

Oddo sighed, and turned back to the house. Maybe he'd find the Little Folk in there.

As he crossed the yard, he saw Grimmr dive on a squirming goat, pick it up and dump it over the fence. The goat gave a mischievous hop and skip and headed straight for a gap in the stones – the gap Grimmr had made when he tried to move the boundary.

'Ha,' thought Oddo. 'Serves you right!'

As the goat bounded past, Oddo had an idea.

'Hey, psst!' The animal clattered to a stop. 'Why don't you head for the mountains?' he suggested. 'There'll be lots of tasty young grass up there. And tell all your friends,' he added, as the goat trotted away.

Oddo reached the house and tiptoed along the passageway. Maybe if he was quiet enough he could take the Little Folk by surprise. He swept the door hangings aside . . .

He'd forgotten how dark it would be indoors. With no lamps or hearthfire, and no windows like Gyda had, the only light in the room was the little patch of sunshine falling through the doorway. Oddo fancied he heard a tiny scuffling sound at the far end of the room, but when he peered at it hopefully, all he could see was shadows.

He lifted the water bucket standing near the door and wrinkled his nose. A layer of scum and dead insects floated on top. Oddo used it to prop open the door hangings and stepped into the gloom. The house didn't feel like home. It was cold and dark and smelt of dead ash and rat droppings. The fur blankets looked strange, all heaped up in a pile ready for the Sheriff. There was no welcoming fire, no scent of cooking. No Bolverk, Sigrid or Hairydog. Not even a sign of the Little Folk. Oddo hurried back to the entrance and squatted in the pool of sunshine next to the tiny table he'd made. It was emptied of every crumb of food. All that lay on it now was a pebble.

Oddo picked up the little stone and twisted it in his fingers. Then he stopped, and stared. Scratched upon the surface, so tiny it was almost invisible, was a mark that looked like a rune.

Oddo felt his heart beating fast. Was it a good rune or a bad rune? Had the Little Folk cast an evil spell on him, or on the house? Were they angry with him for making them do the farmwork?

Oddo scrambled to his feet.

'Runolf will know,' he thought. 'I'll ask Runolf.'

He rushed out of the room, then skidded to a halt.

A procession was climbing the slope from the river: the Thingmen arriving for the land-taking ceremony!

And puffing along behind them was a tubby man

in a flowing, fur-trimmed cloak. Oddo gasped as he recognised the unwelcome figure of the King's Sheriff.

'He's come to collect the taxes,' thought Oddo in dismay. 'And Thora isn't home yet!'

One of Thora's younger brothers was playing on the turf roof when Oddo panted into view. Harald yelled the news down the smoke-hole, and the rest of the family poured out the door to greet him.

'Where's Thora?' they called.

Oddo tried to smile.

'She's coming soon!' he answered. But he knew now it wouldn't be soon enough! He couldn't meet their eager, questioning eyes. 'She said to tell you she just wanted to do something more, and she'll be home in a couple of days with a big bag of silver.'

To his own ears, his cheeriness sounded false, but they all nodded and smiled. 'Good old Thora.'

Only the big sister, the one called Astrid, looked at him with narrowed eyes. She crossed her arms.

'I bet she hasn't got any silver yet,' she hissed in his ear. 'That's why she didn't come back with you, isn't it?'

Oddo ignored her and held out his runestone to Runolf.

'Sir,' he said. 'Could you please tell me what this rune is?'

Raising his eyebrows, Runolf held out his hand. His brows shot even higher at the sight of the little pebble Oddo dropped into his palm.

'How on earth did you come by this?' Runolf exclaimed. 'It's a rune carved by the Little Folk – the most powerful runemakers of all!'

Oddo bit his lip. 'And what does it do?' he asked.

'Why,' said Runolf. 'This is a rune of protection – it protects your home and land.'

Oddo almost collapsed with relief. He could feel his whole body begin to shake as he turned to go home.

'Wait a pickled herring!' cackled Granny Hulda. 'What have you done to your leg, young laddie?'

Oddo was startled. In all the excitement, he'd forgotten about his leg. He looked down.

'I . . . it's injured,' he said.

'Then take yourself inside and let's have a peek at it,' said Granny.

The whole family hustled him towards the house. In a moment he was seated on a bench by the firepit, luxuriating in its comforting warmth. Suddenly he felt weak and shivery, and he realised his leg was hurting badly. He was vaguely aware of someone untying his scruffy, makeshift bandage and pouring warm water over his leg. The wound stung, but it was good to feel the dirt and blood washing away. Granny Hulda slapped on a hot, odorous poultice, and handed him a steaming brew.

'Drink it,' she snapped. 'Willow bark. It'll take away your pain.'

Oddo took a sip and pulled a face. It had a horrid, bitter flavour. But Granny watched him, hands on hips, making sure he emptied the cup.

'I'd better go home now,' he said, attempting to get to his feet. He had to find out what was happening with the King's Sheriff. Maybe he could find a way to delay him till Thora arrived.

'I . . .' He tried to think of an excuse for leaving. 'I've got to see if the animals are all right.'

He felt a hand patting his shoulder and turned to find Ketil regarding him with wide blue eyes. The little boy drew Oddo's head towards his own.

'Your animals are fine,' he whispered, his warm breath tickling Oddo's ear. 'Thora said that someone special was looking after them, but she told me to check on them anyway.'

Oddo stared at him, and gulped.

Thora, Thora, always looking after other people.

'She's out there now searching for the silver so she can save her family,' he thought. He pictured her traipsing along that cold, lonely path, with no fire, no food, and only Hairydog for company – and no idea that all her struggles were going to be in vain. His heart turned over at the thought of her coming back and finding her family thrown out of their home.

ᚺᛗ ᚾᛁᛏᛁ ᚠᛟᚲ

27
Thora and Hairydog

Thora watched till Oddo was out of sight. Then she turned and straightened her shoulders.

'Come on, Hairydog,' she called.

But the dog ignored her, scampering down to the water for a drink. She nosed around the bank and opened her jaws to snap at something.

'Food!' thought Thora. 'When was the last time I had something to eat?!'

She ripped up a handful of dandelion stalks and crammed them into her mouth, swallowing the leaves and flower buds and spitting out the bitter stems. When all the flowers were gone, she knelt down and hacked out their roots, wishing she had a fire to cook them on. Dandelion roots were nice boiled, but raw? She edged down the slippery bank and knelt to rinse one in the river, feeling the strong pull of the current and noticing the height of the water, swollen by the melting snow. She took a nibble of the root and screwed up her nose.

'When I get home,' she promised herself, 'I'll cook pots and pots of yummy, hot food.' At the thought of home, she imagined her family waiting for her to walk in the door with a bag of silver. 'I'd better hurry!' she thought.

She leapt to her feet, forgetting caution, and a moment later she was sliding and bumping down the bank. Before she could even gasp for breath, she plunged into the cold, rushing water.

⟨ᚠᚱᛒ ᚠ ᚱᛚᚾ⟩

28
Taxes for the King

Oddo blinked. He was lying on a hard wooden bench in the house-over-the-hill. That willow-bark brew must have sent him to sleep as well as relieving his pain. He sat up in a fluster. How long had he been here?

Before he could get to his feet, he heard a voice yelling from above, and Harald's head popped down through the smoke-hole.

'Hey, everyone!' warned Harald. 'Look out!'

Next moment the King's Sheriff and his henchmen strode into the room.

'We are here to collect the taxes for King Harald the Fairhair, King of all Norway!' announced the Sheriff.

Runolf, calm and majestic, moved forward and inclined his head.

'We beg your indulgence, good sir,' he said. 'My daughter is at this moment returning from a quest for silver . . .'

'Don't make excuses!' roared the Sheriff. 'You've had time enough to collect your payment. I can't wait for every peasant to laze round upon his bed hoping for silver to drop out of the sky!' His face was flushed and sweaty.

Runolf drew himself up straight.

'Sir,' he said, 'you can accept my word . . .'

'Well, I don't,' said the Sheriff. 'I don't accept anything except taxes. Men!' He turned to his henchmen. They leaned forward, twitching like hunting dogs. 'Search this house,' he ordered. 'Seize anything of value.'

A pointy-nosed man sprang forward and snatched Finnhilda's keys from her belt. Smirking insolently, he bent to open a clothes chest. Granny Hulda sprang at him, the rod she used for spinning clenched in her fist. In a volley of angry squeaks, she walloped the pointy-nosed man on his bottom. He spun round, clutching the seat of his breeches.

Another man began to sidle along the wall in the direction of Runolf's tool chest, but tiny Sissa, reaching it first, clapped her pudgy fingers on the lid. Oddo laughed at the man's astonished expression as he reached the chest and found the keyhole disappearing under a flurry of leaves and flowers.

The Sheriff, his face now purple, pointed at Thora's older brother, Arni.

'Get that able-bodied lad!' he yelled.

Three henchmen turned to look at Arni. Derisive expressions flickered across their faces as they took in his scrawny frame. They rolled up their sleeves and strutted towards him.

Oddo held his breath and watched with glee as Ketil drew on his goatskin hood. The next moment one of the henchmen was crying out with fright and hopping around the room, trying to beat off a very small but invisible attacker.

Meanwhile, little Harald dropped through the smoke-hole onto a rafter. He swung himself along, and pounced, with a bloodcurdling yell, on the second man's head.

There was one assailant left. Arni picked up a rune-stone and twirled it nonchalantly in his fingers. The unsuspecting man reached out to grab his arm. With a gloating smile, Arni flicked his wrist. The henchman flew across the room, hit the wall with a thud, and slithered to the ground.

'Jumping jellyfish!' chuckled Oddo. 'I wouldn't mind one of those runestones!'

Then the Sheriff drew his sword, and Oddo's smile vanished.

'Enough buffoonery!' snarled the Sheriff. 'Surrender

your possessions this instant or I'll burn your house around your ears, I'll . . .'

At that moment, there was a sharp yelp and a creature with wet fur, spiky as pine needles, burst into the room.

Oddo leapt from his seat.

'Hairydog!' he cried.

The next instant the door hangings flew apart again, and a bedraggled, muddy figure appeared in the doorway.

'Thora!'

Thora danced into the room, brandishing a gold chain and a jewelled goblet, then stopped at the chaos that met her eyes.

One man, looking and sounding like a dying sheep, was racing round in circles, tufts of wool hanging off his clothes, while Granny Hulda scuttled after him, whacking him with her distaff rod. Another man was on one leg, hopping all over the room, brandishing a dagger, and apparently trying to cut off his own foot. Someone else was huddled on the floor, holding his head and wailing, while Arni stood flexing his muscles and calling taunts to another man cowering in a corner. The King's Sheriff was in the middle of it all, eyes bulging, sword raised, looking as though he was about to explode.

Oddo, standing on stool by the fire, was the first to see her.

'Hey!' he shouted. 'It's Thora! She's back!'

All eyes turned towards her.

'Ah!' said Runolf, and addressed the Sheriff. 'Let me introduce my daughter Thora. I think I mentioned her . . .'

Thora marched up to the Sheriff and thrust the chain and goblet at him.

'Is this what you're after?' she demanded.

Everyone seemed to hold their breath. The only sounds Thora could hear were the spitting of the flames and the glug-glug of something bubbling in the cooking pot.

The Sheriff let out a loud hiss. He sheathed his sword and held out a shaking hand for the offerings.

'Right,' said Thora. 'Now you can go away!'

The Sheriff tried to look dignified as he stalked out, but his henchmen followed in unseemly haste, hopping and hobbling from the room.

As the door hangings swung behind them, the room rang with cheers.

'Thora!'

'Good old Thora!'

'Thora brought the taxes!'

Bending to hug the invisible child wrapped around her knees, Thora spied Oddo elbowing his way towards her. She grinned at him proudly.

Runolf picked up a chisel and banged it on the table for attention.

'Thora,' he declared, as the shouting dropped to an excited buzz, 'you have vindicated our faith in you!'

Astrid tossed her head disdainfully.

'Huh,' she said, and sniffed.

But for once her sneering only made Thora feel smug.

'Thora!' Oddo was by her side now, tugging at her sleeve. 'How did you get home so quickly? And where on earth did you get that gold and jewel stuff? What happened to the silver?'

'I haven't had a chance to look for it yet,' said Thora, grinning. 'You see, just after you ran off, Ulf turned up, on the way back from his raid.' She paused, re-living the moment when Hairydog had dragged her out of the freezing river, soaked and shivering, and some instinct had prompted her to dig the lucky runestone out of her basket. The next moment, she'd seen that glorious dragon ship, red sail billowing, heading up the fjord towards her. The men had called out to her, begging her to help their wounded. They'd drawn the ship up to shore and rushed round doing her bidding – finding the plants she needed, lighting a fire for her – and all the time heaping her with praise.

'Hey,' said Oddo, waving his hand in front of her eyes and interrupting her reverie. 'So Ulf turned up – so then what?'

'Oh,' said Thora, and she tried to make her voice sound casual. 'I fixed up their wounds, and they paid me with some of their loot! So then, since I had enough to pay the taxes,' she grinned, 'I thought I'd come home in the ship and surprise you. We can look for the silver another day, and maybe I'll keep it and be rich – though I might give a bit to Gyda to make up for tricking her. But Oddo . . .' Her voice began to tremble as the memory came back to her. 'When I got on board I found they had *people* for loot! Men from the strange land – even a boy who looked the same age as us!'

'What for?' asked Oddo.

'They're going to sell them as thralls to work for other people! Don't you think that's awful?'

'Yes,' agreed Oddo.

'And what about you?' Thora exclaimed. 'Did you manage to beat Grimmr home?'

Oddo eyed her solemnly and shook his head.

'No,' he said.

'No?!'

Then Oddo burst into a fit of giggling.

'It didn't matter,' he chortled. 'The Little Folk took care of Grimmr. They opened the door of his barn so all his goats got out, and now he's running around trying to catch them! Come and look.'

A few minutes later, Thora was standing on the other side of the wood, trying to catch her breath and looking round the paddocks for Grimmr and his goats.

'Where are they?' she asked.

Oddo gave a hoot and pointed towards the mountains.

'Look, they listened to me! I told them to go up there.'

Thora looked. Far in the distance she could just make out a running figure. And ahead of him, high on the mountainside, were lots of little moving dots.

'That'll keep him busy for a while!' she cried.

Oddo nodded gleefully.

'In the meantime, I can put all the stones back in the fence. The boundary's got to be in the right place for tomorrow!'

'What about your leg?' asked Thora anxiously. 'Will you be able to walk on it all day? I'd better make you another potion.'

Oddo screwed up his face and shook his head.

'No thanks, I've had enough potions!'

ᛗᚲ ᚦᛚᛋ

29

The ceremony begins

It was still dark when Oddo stepped outside.

'I've made it!' he thought. He shivered with excitement. 'I'm really going to light the needfire and save the farm.'

The Thingmen were waiting, a cluster of dark figures against the lightening sky, and Grimmr was there too, looking tired and rumpled, as if he hadn't slept all night. Oddo grinned.

The Law Speaker held up a stick, and an odd-shaped bow with a floppy string.

'With this drill of ash and this bow of alder, you must light the needfire,' he announced.

Oddo dumped his ball of tinder on the ground, and reached out eagerly for the ash stick and the funny little bow. He eyed the Law Speaker expectantly, waiting for instructions. Around him the air filled with excited voices as people from other farms turned up to watch.

The Law Speaker looked back at Oddo but didn't speak.

Oddo felt a surge of panic. If no one told him what to do, how was he going to light the needfire?

'This puny little earthworm doesn't have a clue!' snorted Grimmr.

The crowd fell silent, and in the expectant hush, Oddo could hear his heart thudding.

He looked desperately at the objects in his hands. Did he rub them together, or what?

Then one of the Thingmen glided towards him. He gestured to the ground where a piece of oak with a notch in its side was lying on a sheet of bark. Silently, he pushed Oddo's shoulder and tapped his knee. A moment later Oddo found himself down on one knee, his left foot standing on the piece of oak. The Thingman stood the drill with its pointy end in the notch, twisted the bowstring around it, then stepped back.

Oddo was left with the bow in one hand, and, in the other, a half-ball of wood, pressed against the top of the drill to hold it steady. He frowned at the bow, bewildered, then gave it a tug. The string pulled, and set the drill spinning.

'That's it!' A wave of relief flooded through him.

He sneaked a glance at Grimmr, who was standing with folded arms, glowering. Then he scrunched up his face and yanked the bow with all the energy he possessed.

'Go on,' he urged himself.

The drill spun, faster and faster. Sawdust flew from the tip and Oddo gulped with excitement as a thin wisp of smoke began to rise.

'Yes! Here comes the fire!'

He felt the crowd press closer in anticipation. The smoke grew thicker and one of the Thingmen lifted his arm. Oddo sucked in his breath and blew at the smoke. A tiny red lump came into sight, glowing in the notch hole. The onlookers cheered and Oddo's heart soared with triumph. He dropped the bow, snatched aside the piece of oak, and stretched out his hand for his ball of tinder. But it was gone! The crowd had trodden on it, scattering it all over the ground. Oddo dived between their legs, frantically scrabbling for the bits of light, dry grass. He grabbed a few wisps and spun back to his ember. But he was too late. The glow had died away.

Oddo flopped on his heels, sick with disappointment. He scowled at the bits of grass lying on his palm, then clenched them fiercely in his fist.

'This time you're going to be where I need you!' he growled.

He shoved them tightly round the notch hole, then picked up the bow again. But now the muscles in his arms and back were too tired. When he tugged the bow, his fingers lost their grip on the drill. It slipped out of the notch and clattered onto the bark. Tears of humiliation sprang to his eyes.

'Grimmr was right,' he thought. 'I can't do this!'

ᛏᛚ ᚲᚱᛟᛏᛗᚲᛏ

30
Ring of fire

At that moment there was a stir in the crowd. Oddo looked up to see Bolverk and Sigrid pushing their way towards him.

'What's going on?' trumpeted Bolverk. 'Why are all these gawpers trampling on my fields?'

Oddo leapt to his feet. 'Grimmr the Greedy's been stealing our land,' he called. 'So I went to the Gula Thing to stop him. They said I have to light a needfire and do a land-taking ceremony to get it back. But . . .' With a choking feeling in his throat, Oddo held out the bow to his father. 'You're home now, so you'd better do it.'

'Bolverk returns in the nick of time!' Grimmr sneered. 'How your little flea of a son imagined he could get a needfire going, I don't know . . . Why, I've heard he can't even fire an arrow!'

Bolverk ignored the bow Oddo was thrusting towards him and glowered at Grimmr. He spoke in a low growl.

'Oddo, son of Bolverk the Bellower, grandson of Frodi the Fearless, is no weakling!' His voice rose to a crescendo. 'My son challenged you, and travelled to the Thing to fight for our land. That is not the action of a weakling!' Bolverk pointed at Oddo, his face flaming. 'Oddo has shown the wits and the bravery of a man. And now he will prove he has the strength of a man! He will light the needfire!'

Fear and exultation poured through Oddo as he looked at his father.

He dropped to his knee, picked up the drill, and took a deep breath. Now not only the fate of the farm rested on his shoulders, but his family's honour as well. And Oddo had a feeling that, in Bolverk's eyes, dignity and respect were even more important than his land.

He wound the string round the drill again, then, clenching the bow in his fist, he gave a careful tug.

'Go on, Oddo,' Bolverk growled, 'you know you can do it.'

This time, the drill stayed in place and began to spin.

Oddo tugged harder, gritting his teeth, forcing his tired muscles to work. He sawed and sawed, till his arm was burning like fire, yearning for that first sign of smoke. He could hear his own breath loud and panting in his ears.

'Go on, Oddo. Go on!' yelled Bolverk.

And suddenly – there it was. A barely visible wisp of grey!

Oddo's arm seemed to pump with a life of its own.

'That's it! That's it!' crowed Bolverk.

Oddo threw down the tools and jerked the oak out of the way. He wrapped the glowing coal in the soft dry tinder and lifted it in his hands. Frantically, he began to blow. Smoke curled upwards. There was a tiny hiss and shower of sparks, then *whoosh*, a spurt of flames shot up from the tinder.

Oddo almost dropped it with shock. He looked round wildly, and the Law Speaker pointed to a ring of stones. Hurriedly, Oddo laid his precious fire in the pit and fed it with the kindling lying ready.

'You have lit the needfire!' proclaimed the Law Speaker. 'You may commence your claim.' He gestured to the bank of the river, and Oddo saw a huge heap of dry branches next to the pile of boundary stones. 'That is the easternmost corner of the land you claim,' continued the Speaker. 'Light your first bonfire there, then proceed around the boundary.' He turned slowly, pointing out more piles of firewood arranged along the fenceline. 'Each of those must be lit by the needfire,' he said, 'till your whole claim is ringed by fire.' He handed Oddo a long bough of crab-apple. 'Now begin.'

Oddo held the bough over his little needfire, till the end burst into flame. Glowing with a pride as fierce as the flame, he rose to his feet and faced his father. Bolverk was beaming back at him.

Oddo carried the flaming torch of the apple bough high above his head, and people cheered, just as he'd imagined. Hairydog pattered by his side, her head cocked proudly.

Oddo bent to light the first bonfire.

'Remember,' warned the Law Speaker, 'you must return before the sun sets and before the first bonfire expires. Should you fail, this land will go to the other claimant.'

Oddo hurried along the river bank. At the next pile of boundary stones, he kindled the heap of firewood and looked over his shoulder. The fire behind him was still blazing brightly. He turned away from the river and took a deep breath. It was a long uphill trek now, up to the high summer pastures in the foothills of the mountains. Oddo set off at a fast pace. People dotted around the fields called out words of encouragement, and he grinned back at them.

To his right he could see the land where Grimmr farmed, and the hayshed filled with stolen hay. Grimmr was standing in the doorway of his house, gazing down the slope, and the scowl on his face made Oddo glance behind him. No wonder Grimmr was furious! Oddo felt a surge of triumph. The bonfires he'd lit were forming a ring around his land, just as the Law Speaker had said. The sight spurred him forward.

But as the sun rose higher, and the ground grew steeper, each pile of firewood seemed further than the one before. Oddo paused and squinted up the slope, searching for the next heap of branches. His heart sank when he spied it, so small and distant it looked like a bird's nest. He felt something hot blowing on his hand and glancing at the apple bough, he saw with alarm that it had burnt down to a short stump. He mustn't let it die away! Racing up the hill towards the closest tree, he wrenched off a branch and held it anxiously over the needfire. When it caught alight he heaved a sigh of relief and set off, feeling very pleased with himself.

The glow of pride lasted just two steps. With a clutch of dread, Oddo realised that he'd failed to ask the tree's permission before he tore off a limb.

'No! Now I'll have bad luck!' he groaned.

Almost at once, his injured leg began to throb. As he set off for the next pile of firewood, he felt the blood oozing through his bandage. With every step, pain shot through his leg. He thought with longing of Thora's healing leaves and that foul willow-bark brew. He clenched his teeth and forced himself to keep moving, one foot in front of the other. In the sky, the sun reached its peak and slowly, relentlessly, began to descend.

Every few minutes Oddo lifted his weary head and

glanced hopefully towards the high mountain pastures. Would he never reach them?

He felt dizzy and confused. On one side of him, among the trees, he seemed to keep glimpsing the shape of a wolf. Was it Grey Wolf keeping him company? Or was it one of the magic wolves he'd made with his wolfspell? His mind was whirling. He had to struggle to remember where he was going and what he was trying to do. He reached another bonfire and found his way blocked by a huge heap of boundary stones. He stared at it, perplexed, before he realised what it meant.

'I'm at the top!' he cried. 'I'm halfway round!' He turned the corner, his spirits rising. 'I just have to cross this field, then it's downhill for the rest of the way.'

But as he shifted weight to his wounded leg, he felt a wave of nausea and pain.

Thora stood at the edge of the wood and peered into the distance.

'I thought as much!' she muttered when Oddo came into sight. 'He's limping!'

She watched him stumbling down the hill, wearily shifting the torch from hand to hand. Then she smiled down at the jar of potion she was keeping warm, wrapped in a corner of her apron.

When she looked at Oddo again, he was dragging his feet as if he were struggling through a bog. The torch slipped from his hand and lay burning on the ground, but Oddo just stood there swaying, and looking at it. Thora glared at the pink glow spreading over the sky, sure the sun had never sunk so fast before.

'Oddo!' she called, and started to run towards him.

'Halt!' cried a fierce voice.

Startled, Thora glanced over her shoulder. A tall Thingman was striding towards her, waving his arms.

'Halt!' he said again.

Thora stopped uncertainly.

'No other person is allowed near the claimant!' he boomed.

Thora held up the jar.

'But . . . I just want to give him this potion. For his sore leg,' she explained.

To her dismay, the Thingman shook his head. Thora sucked in her breath in frustration and turned back to Oddo.

The shouting had caught his attention and he was gazing dazedly in her direction.

'Come on, Oddo,' she yelled. 'The sun's setting. Hurry up!'

To her relief, her words seemed to work like a swig of potion. Oddo turned to look at the sky behind him and Thora could see the shock on his face as he bent down to scoop up the torch. She watched with her heart in her mouth as he began to totter forward again. His face was drained of colour, and there was fresh blood soaking through his breeches.

Then Oddo saw something that brought a look of panic to his face. He gave a cry and began to run. Spinning round, Thora saw that the first bonfire had nearly died away.

There was a thud, and a moan rose from the watching crowd. Thora swung back to see Oddo sprawled on the ground, his face in the dirt.

'Oddo!' she screamed. 'Oddo! Oddo!'

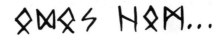

31

Sunset

Oddo felt something slippery under his hand. He opened his eyes and stared in surprise at a slimy puddle of blood on the ground. There was a ringing in his ears, but he fancied he could hear the distant sound of voices calling.

'Oddo! Oddo! Oddo!'

Painfully, he lifted his head. A ring of Thingmen seemed to be standing around him, but they ebbed and flowed like waves on a beach. Behind them bobbed other faces, with staring eyes and gaping mouths. And then his glance fell on one face that was wearing a huge leering grin, a face with a bald shining dome. Grimmr's face!

Oddo's head cleared and he looked round in a panic

for the needfire. It lay just out of reach, a fading spark in a stump of blackened branch.

'No!' cried Oddo.

He threw himself across the ground and picked it up, blowing frantically to get some life out of the feeble glow.

'Move back! Move back!' ordered the Thingmen, pushing at the crowd to clear his way.

Oddo tried to rise to his feet, but to his dismay his injured leg wouldn't take his weight. He lay on his front staring helplessly down the hill. The bonfire he'd lit this morning was only a pile of embers, while the water of the river glowed red in the light of the setting sun. Painfully, he began to crawl down the slope. He struggled to hold up the torch so it wouldn't scrape along the ground, but the stump had burnt so low, the flame was scorching his fingers. In a moment he'd be forced to drop it, and then his fight would be over.

'I've failed!' he thought. 'Grimmr will get our land!'

He glanced at the crowd waiting on the riverbank. He saw Thora gazing at him, willing him not to give up. He seemed to hear her voice whispering in his ear.

'Go on, Oddo!' it urged. 'You made a wolfspell. You can do anything!'

Suddenly, a last desperate idea exploded in his mind. Before he could speak, Hairydog seemed to sense what he wanted and streaked across the paddock for the house. She burst back into view, a bow and arrow clenched between her jaws and thrust them at Oddo. He dropped the needfire to the ground, grabbed the arrow and held it to the flame.

'Come on,' he urged. 'Come *on*!'

The dry wood of the arrow burst into a blaze and Oddo gave a whoop of triumph. Elation lent him a moment of strength. He rose to his knees and fitted the flaming arrow to the bow. Then his heart turned over. With fire roaring along the shaft, how was he going to judge the shot? And he only had one chance to get it right! With churning belly, he drew back the string, squinted along his arm, and fired.

The crowd fell silent, all heads turning in unison as the flare of light arced through the air. There was a gasp as it dropped towards the dying fire, and then a roar as it landed right in the middle, with a spurt of flame.

'I did it!' cried Oddo. 'I did it! I got the needfire back before the sun set and before the bonfire died!'

But in front of the flames . . . Oddo blinked in disbelief. There seemed to be a little man no bigger than a bird beckoning in agitation. And Grimmr, his face contorted with rage, was stabbing his hand in Oddo's direction.

'Oh no,' Oddo realised in panic, '*I've* got to get there too!' He cast a glance behind him. The last red was fading from the sky. 'I'm coming!' he yelled.

He threw himself on the ground and began to roll, faster and faster, down the slope. In no time at all he crashed to a halt – just in front of the bonfire.

His father was leaning over him, with the biggest, proudest grin Oddo had ever seen spreading across his face. Then Bolverk straightened up and turned to Grimmr.

'Did I hear you claim,' Bolverk demanded, 'that Oddo couldn't even fire an arrow?'

Grimmr snorted in reply, but Oddo didn't hear. His eyes were fixed upon a tiny man, clad in cobwebs and moss, who winked at him and waved his hand before he darted out of sight behind the flames.

The Futhark

To read or write words written in runes, you have to go by the *sound* they make. These are the rune sounds:

ᚠ	f	ᛁ	i (as in *it*) or i (as in *ice*)
ᚢ	oo or u (as in *up*)	ᚹ	p
ᚦ	th	ᛉ	z
ᚨ	a	ᛋ	s
ᚱ	r	ᛏ	t
ᚲ	k	ᛒ	b or v
ᚷ	g	ᛖ	e
ᚹ	w	ᛗ	m
ᚺ	h	ᛚ	l
ᚾ	n	ᚴ	ng
ᛁ	ee	ᛞ	d
ᛃ	j or y (as in *yes*)	ᛟ	o

Can you work out why the alphabet is called the Futhark?

Writing your name in runes will give you some magic powers, but the Futhark doesn't match the English alphabet exactly. Some English words can't be written in runes.

Want to send a message to the author?
Or discover some of the secrets
behind the making of *Wolfspell*
and the other Viking Magic books?
Then visit www.viking-magic.com